WORTH THE WAIT

LAKE SPARK
BOOK 3

EVEY LYON

ABOUT

Ford Spears, star hockey player, is ready to grab the only goal he has ever wanted—a second chance with the mother of his child.

For our son. That's the explanation my hockey-playing ex gave as to why we need to spend time as a family at his lake house in the small town where it all began. What I didn't expect was to show up and discover our son is spending another week at camp, and Ford and I are all alone. Oh, and he wants me to fake a relationship for a day to fulfill an old lady's wish too. I realize that Ford is on the mission that I always feared...

He wants to win me back.

But our past is filled with heartache and regrets. It's going to take a lot more than a few strolls down memory lane or romantic boat rides on the lake. And don't get me started on the man refusing to wear a shirt around the house. He wants us to have one week together and pretend we could have it all, and I know it's not a good idea. Not when I'm not sure who believes in us more, because we are both wondering if together, we were always worth the wait.

Ford and Brielle bring the feels and steam in this completely swoon-worthy forced-proximity second-chance love story. Worth the Wait is book three in the complete standalone interconnected Lake Spark *series. For lovers of small-town romance with a touch of sports.*

WORTH THE WAIT PLAYLIST

1. My Sweet Baby by Thieving Birds
2. Don't Give Up On Me by Zach Bryan
3. Name by The Goo Goo Dolls
4. The Freshman by The Verve Pipe
5. Collide by Howie Day
6. Brick by Ben Folds Five
7. Bigger Than The Whole Sky by Taylor Swift
8. Around Again by Hovvdy
9. Anti-Hero (country version) by Josiah & the Bonnevilles
10. High Beams by Zach Bryan
11. Glue Myself Shut by Noah Kahan
12. Thumbs by Zander Hawley
13. Oh My Heart by R.E.M.

FORD

Don't look at her fingers. I'll regret it if I do.

First, I will admire the way Brielle swipes a few strands of her silky brown hair away from her cheek, and then I will follow the line of her jaw until I stare at her soft lips that always curve in a soft smile when she talks about Connor, our son. And finally, the pièce de résistance, her hands. And it's why I'm going to regret locking my gaze on her fingers, because there is something missing from her ring finger, and it's all my fault.

Man, I know I'm torturing myself.

I look.

I get lost for a second—okay, maybe two.

"Mr. Spears, wouldn't you agree?" A lady's voice breaks my turmoil.

Blinking my eyes a few times, I look forward and see my son's soon-to-be-retired teacher smiling at me from the other side of the table for our end-of-year parent-teacher meeting. I only glance for a second, as my sight whips back in Brielle's direction, where she's sitting beside me. Brielle Dawson or

Elle to me, mother of my child, the most beautiful woman I've ever known, and the only one I've seen a future with.

But the chance was ripped away from us ten years ago because of a promise.

"Ford, are you okay?" Brielle double-checks with me; her blue eyes have a curious glint in them.

I clear my throat, remembering what we were talking about. "Of course, we'll make sure he keeps reading over the summer."

"I know Connor is excited for hockey camp, and I hope he enjoys it, but it's important he arrives to the fifth grade ready. It's his last year before middle school," Mrs. Clark reminds me.

Brielle gently touches my arm. "We will be sure to get the books on the summer reading list," she assures the teacher.

Mrs. Clark brings her hands together. "Wonderful. I just wanted to say that, despite his little outburst recently, he is a sweet boy, and I will miss him."

My jaw tightens about the reminder of a few weeks ago when he had an argument with a classmate. Glancing to Brielle, I see her strained look.

"You two should be proud of him, and if I may say so, be proud of yourselves too," Mrs. Clark adds.

"How so?" I wonder.

"I can't tell you how many times I've had these meetings go south when the parents are separated, and their child has issues in class because of their parents' behavior toward each other."

Brielle taps her nails on the table and throws on a tight smile. "That's not us." She takes a deep breath. "We only want the best for Connor."

Fuck me, how is it years later, and I still hear the sadness drenched in that sentence?

"Thank you for the compliment." I awkwardly attempt to stay calm. "If Connor hasn't said anything at school, then I guess we're doing a good job."

The teacher's smile falters slightly. "If I may be frank…"

"Please." My tone is clipped.

"He's all smiles when he talks about you both. Not many kids can say they have a famous hockey star as their dad. But sometimes he mentions that you both live in two different worlds and only ever come together at set times, and he knows it's because of him."

Brielle's breath cuts short, and she looks off into the distance out the window.

I swipe a hand through my hair that's still short from hockey season. "Kids are intuitive, aren't they?" I say in a flat tone, not so amused.

Mrs. Clark laughs awkwardly. "They are. Well…" She glances between us. "That's everything. I wish you both a great summer."

Brielle offers a polite smile. "You too, and thank you for ensuring Connor had a great school year."

We all stand and say our goodbyes.

Brielle and I take the longest walk in silence out of the school and to our cars that are side by side in the parking lot. I know something is weighing heavy on her mind because my own thoughts feel like a brick too.

We both hit the unlock buttons on our key fobs, yet neither one of us makes a move to climb in the driver's side. Instead, we face one another, with the late-afternoon sun on full blast.

Our eyes lock and so begins our usual lingering gaze.

It happens every damn time.

Every drop-off, pick-up, birthday party, meals we have together as a family for Connor's sake, every time she brought Connor to my games to watch, and I would catch her staring as I glided by on the ice.

It's all a fucking simmer that never boils over.

"That went well," she notes and nibbles her bottom lip.

I throw my sunglasses on because I need protection from staring at her blue floral-print summer dress with an annoying button loose at the top. The dress deserves to be hanging off the edge of my bed because it was thrown off in a moment of clarity.

"It always does. Parenting we're good at."

She snorts a cute little laugh. "I would say we aren't that bad. She had to bring up the other week, didn't she?"

A sound escapes my mouth as I debate if I can tease her about this or not. "It will go down as memorable."

Her hand finds her hip. "Easy for you to say, you were the one who had to deliver the news to me."

I hold my hands up in surrender. "I was put in an awkward position, thanks. Not easy for either one of us."

"Connor asked you to deliver the news that I'm no longer allowed to write notes in his lunch."

"Elle, he's getting a little old for that, and when someone bothered him at school about it, then yeah, he thought it would be better if I talked to you to deliver the message of no more notes. Along with the need to no longer pre-slice his apples. Trust me, I feared that conversation with you all day." I can't control my smile at this.

She throws on a fake pout that is too fucking adorable. "I can't handle him growing so fast." We're still young ourselves.

"Kids tend to grow up. If you're missing having a baby, then I can volunteer my services again," I joke, but the humor hits a little too close to home.

Her smile stills, unsure even, and it's a good few seconds

before her tone turns serious. "Should we be worried about what Mrs. Clark mentioned about the set-time-togetherness thing?" She whirls her fingers in the air.

My head lolls to the side. "Maybe."

"I guess we should have a look at the schedule again since you'll no longer have games."

Ouch, that reminder.

The season that just ended was my last as a professional hockey player as the center and captain of the Chicago Spinners, thanks to age and one injury too many. Nothing major, but I don't recover the way I did ten years ago when I was twenty. I feel a shade of pain spread on my face.

And she knows me so well, as she studies me with a knowing wry smile. "Going to miss it, huh?"

I shrug a shoulder. "It was my life for so long, but yeah, I'm good. I have a plan B, been planning it for a few seasons now."

"Right, the new sports training facility near Lake Spark."

I chuckle to myself at the way she says Lake Spark, as if it's a mystical place that she fears in a funny kind of way.

During hockey season, I was on the road and stayed at hotels in the city. In my downtime, I escaped to Lake Spark in upstate Illinois. The place I remember from my childhood, through summers as a teenager with a particular brunette, and now it's the place where I fully intend to make a life post-hockey career.

Brielle lives in Hollows, a perfect middle point between Chicago and Lake Spark. She's always had Connor for most of the year, since I had training and game seasons.

"I enjoy it there. You still need to see my house again now that it's finally finished, and you can see if you approve of Connor's room. The interior designer did a good job, I think."

She waves a hand at me. "When it comes to our son, then you know I trust you."

"Still, you can't avoid Lake Spark." I reach out to touch her shoulder, to both comfort her and grab an opportunity to touch her skin because I know she'll tolerate it.

She tilts her head to the side and allows her cheek to nuzzle into my wrist near her shoulder. It's a throwback to a time when we could have had everything. Through the years she occasionally does this, reminding me of the trust we have with one another, the connection we will always share, and the reminder that a different ending floats in our minds.

"I'm not avoiding Lake Spark. I'm just debating what to remember." Her voice is delicate.

I step closer to her, and I move my hand to her cheek to brush my thumb along the stretch of soft skin on her cheekbone. "Everything," I say huskily.

Something must strike in her mind because she attacks her bottom lip, and she steps back. "So, uhm, I guess you have Connor for the first few weeks of summer vacation, and I know he'll enjoy hockey camp one of those weeks." She is changing the subject.

Her avoidance of topics causes me to smirk. "Yeah, we'll be fine, like always. Are you ready?"

"Studying for the Bar exam is a job in itself. I'm lucky I could give up my part-time paralegal job. Thanks for changing the schedule so I have some alone time to study."

A proud smile takes over me. She's been waiting for this. College took longer because Connor was a surprise, then she had LSATs and law school. It was the plan and dream she always wanted, and now it's within her grasp.

"You'll nail it. And you take all the time you need…" I remember she mentioned Illinois only has the exam twice a year. I want her to succeed, which is probably why it spits out of my mouth. "I've got Connor covered and can bump up child support if you need."

The moment it slips off my lips, she raises a brow at me and gives me a stern look. But she isn't mad. She shakes her head at me, entertained. "We're fine." Her pride is strong, or rather, she will never ask for more because I know she appreciates the generous child support I give; it's to cover her needs too. She reaches out to gently shove my shoulder. "Look at you, Mr. Big Shot Retired Hockey Star with millions."

"If only I had it all," I say it in jest, but the truth is underlying.

I may have the house, the money, the car, and a great kid, but I don't have her.

A car slowly drives by, reminding us that we're in a parking lot.

"I should probably go. Connor's at a friend's having a sleepover, and I promised to meet someone for drinks."

I tense. "Someone," I mutter.

Clearly not quietly enough, as Elle chortles a sound. "Another mom from school. Lena, you know her."

Rolling my eyes, I remind myself that I knew that. Connor makes it a point to tell me which single dads are swimming in close waters to Elle at school pickup, because even my kid tries to light fire under my ass.

I nod once. "Have fun then. I'll text Connor later."

"I know. You always do."

Damn straight. Even when it was hockey season and I was traveling for games, I texted every day.

"My sister will pick him up for camp on Friday since I have a meeting," I remind her.

"Is Violet excited to help out with camp?"

I grin to myself. My sister is in college studying business, so I offered her a summer job to do administration. "Excited may be a stretch, but she is appreciative, I think, and it will be good for her resume."

"I bet. Just warn her that when she picks up Connor, I'll be out back probably bawling my eyes out that he's going to camp. You know how it goes." She grins as she says that.

I scratch my cheek. "Yeah, I do."

"Well, I should go. Text me if I need to pack anything special, I just figured you have the hockey equipment thing sorted out." Her hands make gestures in the air because she seems unsure what to do.

I give her a little salute. "Yes, ma'am."

She playfully swats me in passing, and I pretend to be hurt. But that's us. Incredibly comfortable with each other.

I truly believe it's because I'm her guy, and she won't let anyone else have a slither of the connection that we have. She just doesn't admit it.

I watch her for an extra second as she gets in her car to leave, very much aware that this feeling of wanting her is more apparent now because my life is changing. The rush of hockey is gone, which means that underlying feeling is louder than ever. I have no more distractions.

I also remember every day over the years how I wanted this to be our time.

———

FIVE MINUTES LATER, I'm on the road heading back to Lake Spark, the small town that most people find charming and quaint, but it's been the backdrop to my life for every good and bad memory. Zach Bryan is playing on my stereo while, as per usual, Brielle lingers in my mind.

It's so damn simple.

We haven't been together since before Connor was born.

Then the first years with Connor, we were overwhelmed, or rather Brielle took the brunt of newborn life while I was off playing hockey, and by the time the baby years were gone, and Brielle was on her way with college, then that became the focus. I was at the height of my career, and I barely saw them half of the year. There were also those few years I played in Nashville, only to be traded back to Chicago. It's only in the last year or two that we found a pattern with Connor who's no longer a baby and is fairly easy, but by then, the distance between Brielle and me had been created, except for… those moments.

God, those moments.

Always there but now more frequent.

She would take Connor to a few of my home games and watch me, and the times when we briefly talk after I drop Connor off, and I always swipe her hair behind her ear while her eyes sparkle in a way I swear is only for me.

We have been looming in the inevitable. I knew my days of playing hockey were numbered, and there were no more years of preparing for the Bar for Brielle.

Nothing is in our way except us.

I'm bursting, ready to snap.

Either I find some miracle to keep myself in line or this is where ten years in the making shatters and sends us in a new direction, one where I finally do something about us.

My car speaker informs me I have an incoming call, and I hit the button on my steering wheel.

"Hey, buddy," I say, looking at the caller ID. My neighbor and friend Spencer is on the other end. "Shouldn't you be throwing balls or something?" I tease him, as he's a pitcher for the Chicago Bluelights.

"Yeah, yeah, yeah. I just wanted to check in on how it

went. We know how you get after seeing Brielle, and I'm not around to offer you a beer since I have a game."

I turn onto the next road. "The usual. Nothing is going to change. We made a promise, and I don't see that changing anytime soon."

Spencer scoffs a sound of disapproval. "You know you can't avoid the obvious forever, right? I mean, hockey is no longer a roadblock, that's for sure."

I sigh. "It's complicated." I repeat this mantra on a daily basis, and now I'm telling Spencer.

"Doesn't have to be."

My jaw flexes, as I always tense when I think about the possibilities, partly because it feels so close. "We kind of dug ourselves a hole."

"Then climb on out of it," he urges.

I groan because I've been contemplating what I can do. We have seven and a half more years before Connor is eighteen, which means seven and a half years of limbo with his mother while we are responsible for his life as a minor.

We both see what we want, but we say nothing. What are we waiting for? The cards have changed.

My phone beeps, letting me know that someone else is trying call.

"As thrilling as this conversation is, I have someone else trying to reach me right now. I'll call you later."

He agrees, and I quickly answer the next call. I didn't look at the screen, but as soon I hear the other voice say hello, I know it's Margo.

"Hey, Margo." She's the closest thing to a grandmother I have, a close family friend who may have dated my grandfather before he passed, we're not sure, but they were good friends and he was a widower. She's pushing her early eighties, and although mostly healthy, Illinois winters are too harsh for her arthritis, so she's moving to Florida soon. "To what do I owe the pleasure?" I smile because every conversation with her is upbeat.

"I ran into your neighbor the other day at the general store," she begins.

"Which neighbor?"

"The sporty one."

I laugh. "That doesn't help, I live next to a football coach and a pitcher."

"The one with a kid."

"Again, not narrowing the field. Hudson has a baby and an adult son, and Spencer has a daughter a little younger than Connor." I focus on the road although it's mostly clear up ahead.

"With the young girlfriend or wife."

Blowing out a breath, I chuckle. "Okay, we're going in circles. They both have that, so my guess is that it's Spencer, since April drags him to the grocery store at every chance since she's into cooking."

"Yes! He did mention recipes. Anyhow, he doesn't hold it in, and we chatted about you and how you *maybe* need to rethink your priorities on a few things."

"I'm sure you did." No enthusiasm seeps through my tone.

"The thing is, I have my birthday coming up, and I have a small request."

"I'm not sure what else you would want." She lives a life where money is no issue.

Margo hums a sound. "Are you driving? You may want to pull over…"

And a few minutes later, it clicks how this really is my moment of opportunity.

Because I'm done waiting when it comes to Brielle.

2

BRIELLE

Glancing down at my floral-print dress, I shake my head at myself that I purposely undid one button at the top. Grabbing my glass of Chardonnay, I internally berate myself for the button move, knowing I did it because I was going to see Ford today.

"You seem kind of out of sorts," my friend Lena tells me. "It was a Ford day, wasn't it?"

I notice she smiles to herself as she drags her brown hair to the side. We are sitting at the bar while we wait for our table to be ready. It's a chic enough restaurant, but then again, everything in our small town of Hollows is decorated with perfection, down to the lighting hanging over our heads.

"Yeah, it was. I think it's worse now. I mean, now we don't have another hockey season looming over us." I take a sip.

"And hockey is what kept you two in line? I really don't get you guys." She grabs some nuts from the small bowl.

"It's complicated."

She scoffs a sound at me. "Enlighten me."

"You know the story. I was eighteen, unexpectedly pregnant, and being together wasn't really…" I can't even explain it.

Lena affectionately touches my shoulder. "That was then. You're telling me through the years, the opportunity didn't arise for you and Ford?"

"No." I'm firm on my answer. "For so many reasons. Hockey pretty much ruled the schedule, and I couldn't even imagine being in a relationship around that. I had law school to focus on. Plus, we both tried to move on."

"How did that go for you?" She raises a brow at me with a knowing look.

"Well… I've dated, so has Ford." And it was excruciating on all counts and a big-time failure.

"Yet you are both still alone."

"Doesn't mean we should try being together. We have Connor to think about, it's way too risky." And my heart can't handle another heartbreak with Ford involved.

He already affects me enough; I can't even imagine what it would be like to feel as though our possibilities could become a reality.

"I'm just saying you shouldn't be getting butterflies in your stomach at every parent-teacher meeting and pick-up or drop-off. I see my ex and feel blank, nothing."

I nudge her shoulder with my own. "That's because you now have a hot professor to occupy your life." Her ex-college sweetheart is now her fiancé after reconnecting after her divorce.

She clinks my glass with hers. "That I do. Which also proves the point that second chances are not a fairytale."

I play with the stem of my wine glass, trying to shake Ford out of my head. It's a hard task since summer Ford is an extra dose of handsome. Even all these years later, his skin warms well with the summer light, and he keeps his tall, slim figure in shape, even if he isn't training, and God, his brown eyes complement his matching hair that I know he'll start to grow since it's the summer months.

It's the shape of his shoulders that I like to look at the most. They're broad, but the curves remind me of the way he used to hold me, the nights I would lie in his arms, and the time I leaned against him as I cried for hours.

Lena snaps her fingers in front of me. "Holy cow, you're lost in Ford thoughts again. I can tell by your face; you are dreaming away."

"Ahh, okay, you're right. I guess the meeting today is still fresh in my head. I will be back to normal by the main course, I promise."

She hops off the stool. "I'll hold you to that. Be right back, need a ladies' room stop before dinner."

"Sure. I'll order those mozzarella sticks you promised me." My favorite by far. She offers me a warm smile.

Sighing, I look into my wine glass before taking a drink, thankful that Lena is the designated driver tonight.

"You're too pretty to have a frown on your face." A deep man's voice grabs my attention, and I look up to see a man in a suit at the bar. I didn't notice him before. He looks a few years older than me, and admittedly, he isn't bad on the eyes. I can tell the gel in his hair makes his hair seem darker than it is.

"Oh, just a weekday reflection. Nothing a deep breath and a glass of wine can't fix."

He indicates with his fingers in the air for the barman to come to him. "I know how it goes. Luckily, I use the train rides back from the city to clear my head, but I need a drink before I work on a deposition until the early hours."

"You're a lawyer?"

"I am." He nods to the barman. "A whiskey neat, and the

lady will have…"

I shake my head. "Oh, nothing. Thank you. I'm here with a friend."

"Let me know if you change your mind." The corner of his mouth hitches up.

I smile politely. "What kind of law do you practice?"

"Corporate. Does that interest you?" He has a suave grin.

"Actually, I'm sitting the Bar this summer. I finished law school at the university here in Hollows."

"No way." He slides to the free stool next to me. "That's my alma mater. What kind of law do you want to practice?"

"Family law or property, I think."

He thanks the barman for his whiskey. "That area would suit you."

I have a conspicuous grin. "What makes you say that?"

"You have a soft face." He seems proud of his comment. "I'm Brody, by the way."

"Brielle."

"That's a beautiful name." I swear he is investigating my lack of rings on my fingers.

"I hate it sometimes. Nobody knows how to shorten it, Bri or Elle or even Rie."

"All still nice names."

I feel Lena return as she touches my back. "Our table still isn't ready?" She notices that I seem to be in conversation. "Ooh, he's a looker and hopefully single for you. *A distraction,*" she mutters under her breath.

I shoot her a warning glare, but Brody seems to have heard. "I don't want to interrupt your dinner plans, but here…" He reaches into his suit pocket to pull out a card and offers it to me. "Maybe you would like to meet up to discuss law, Brielle?"

Lena nearly chokes, probably because we both know that

was not what he means—or maybe he does. My flirting skills are a bit rusty. "Take the card." She utters her suggestion with an overdone smile.

Hesitating for a few seconds, I can't tear my sight off the card, reminding myself that I'm not taken, need a diversion even, and my fingers flex out.

"Or not." Lena yanks my arm out of nowhere. "Ex."

"What?" I look to her and see her eyes are blazing with shock.

"Hockey baby daddy, nine o'clock," Lena whispers.

At the speed of light, my head whips in the direction of the door where I see Ford standing there with a steely look, hands hanging at his sides and forming into fists. His jaw flexes, and judging by the fact he is storming in our direction, then I know he witnessed the last minute.

"Ford?" I'm confused as to why he's here.

He is quick to bring his arm to the back of my chair, as if he needs to make a claim, and his eyes land on Brody who left the card on the bar.

"What are you doing here?" I ask him.

"You know this guy? He's Ford Spears, a hockey legend." Brody seems surprised and looks at me, as if suddenly I'm an alien. "You watch hockey?"

"Oh…" I nervously tuck a strand of hair behind my ear, as that is the connection Brody is making to Ford. "Actually   "

"Elle is the mother of my child which makes me the father of her child, so we *are* connected." Ford flashes a victorious smile, with his eyes seeing red.

Protective Ford is a force not to be messed with, and it's oddly sexy as hell.

Rolling my eyes, I sigh, as I know there is only one way out of this. "Excuse us. It was nice to meet you," I tell Brody who has a neutral look because he seems to recognize that Ford and I have a delicate relationship, to put it mildly.

I grip Ford's shirt sleeve and yank him with me as I head to the door and out onto the sidewalk of Main Street.

Turning to him, I don't know what to think. "What are you doing here, Ford? I thought you were going back to Lake Spark?"

His eyes stay glued to me, not blinking, while his feet stay firmly planted. "I'm clearly saving you from men in suits who are only after one thing."

I scoff in disbelief that this is where our conversation is heading. "Not that it's any of your business but I was waiting for Lena, and he was just making small talk, he's a lawyer."

"A man giving his card to a woman looking like you do in that dress is not making small talk."

"What's wrong with my dress?" I step closer to him and poke his chest with my finger. "You have some nerve."

He is quick to defend. "When it comes to you, yeah, I do."

I could cut the air with a knife. He knows how to break down my defenses because I cherish the idea that he feels he has a claim to me.

I drop my finger and blow out a breath as I gather my thoughts, and I realize that I still don't have my answer. "Why are you here?"

IIe pinches the bridge of his nose, clearly agitated. "Would you have taken his card?"

I fold my arms over my chest. "What? I don't know. Maybe. To be polite."

It's the truth, maybe he would be the key to forgetting about you.

Ford scrubs his face with his hand. "Don't be polite."

I shake my head because we'll go in a circle. "Answer me

as to why you're here."

He tilts his head to the side and licks his lips. "I've been thinking about what Connor's teacher said."

"Oh." My heart pinches.

"I think it's a point we needed to hear, maybe we should be putting in more effort."

"What more can we do?"

"Summer vacation, we should spend time together, the three of us."

My eyes grow big, and my mouth opens but no words come out. I feel my throat go dry, and I swallow. "Like a family trip or something?"

"Something like that. Why don't you come stay at my place after Connor's hockey camp finishes? A little lake time, all three of us." There is so much conviction in his voice that I know he believes his suggestion is a plausible solution.

A gasp escapes me. "You're serious?"

"Very."

I step to the side as I take in the last minute. "I'm not sure it's a good idea."

It's really not.

It would mean more time with Ford, memories of our younger selves, and the confrontation that Ford is no longer married to hockey.

Ford is quick to grab my arm to draw me back to him, ensuring our eyes meet. "It's an excellent idea. We've had family dinners together, but this is something more and for him. Showing Connor that we are all one team."

"One team." I huff a laugh because this isn't what I imagined calling my dream family.

"He needs this, Elle," he pleads.

"I… I don't know." I'm doubtful. *Very* doubtful.

There is a pause as we both stand there as two former

lovers trying to find our road forward.

We both promised to always put Connor first, and that's my inner turmoil at this very second. Do I ignore the warning signs if it means putting Connor first?

"Margo… it's her birthday, and she's asking that you visit." He adds fuel to the fire.

"Ford…" What do I say to that? Margo did so much for us. She stood up for us when nobody else would.

"We owe her."

I blow out a long breath. "I know."

"Is it so bad that we give a little time for Connor and Margo?"

I look at him like he's crazy. "You know it's not just that."

Do I need to spell out all the reasons this is a bad idea? His heated look is reason one, and my jumping heart is reason two.

"Come on, Elle, neither one of us will be able to sleep knowing we could give Connor a week to help ensure he knows all is okay."

"You're right. It's just…"

He catches my gaze and places his hands on my shoulders so I can't escape. "You can have your own room… if you want." Ford's swaggered-mischief ways cause me to smirk, but I still give him wide eyes. "You can study and relax whenever. We can take Connor to places together on your breaks."

I should be more focused when studying, but Ford is presenting an offer to consider.

"I mean, I guess a little family time would be reasonable."

"Then agree."

I puff out a breath. This isn't going to be my smartest move, but it's for Connor. "Okay."

Ford's long finger brushes my cheek. "Good."

My face is blank. "You hunted me down instead of calling?"

He grins. "Of course, you're easier to sway when we're face to face."

It's because I melt a little inside every time I see you.

"Is Lena driving you home or do you need me to drive you?"

My thighs tighten from the thought of being stuck in a car with him. I know he would walk me to my door, and because I hate the idea of him driving back in the dark, then I would offer him the sofa and drive myself crazy.

My voice nearly croaks. "I'm good."

I kick a small pebble on the ground and cross my arms over my chest, shaking my imagination away and focusing on his request for family time. "But Ford, let's just remember that… we had a plan." Agreed on long ago.

He exhales loudly. "Plans can change."

His statement stirs something inside of me, hope mixed with fear.

Gently I tip my head up to acknowledge that I heard him. "Night," I say.

When I walk away, every ounce of me knows he is right. Plans *can* change. But that doesn't mean they should.

By the time I'm back inside, Lena is at our table for dinner, and I join her.

She props her chin up on her hand as she patiently waits for me to explain.

"I just agreed to spend a week of family holiday time at Ford's lake house." I take a long breath.

Lena smirks as she holds up the card from Brody and ceremonially rips it in two. "I don't think we will be needing this then, like *ever*."

"I'm in way over my head," I say, admitting defeat.

3

BRIELLE

I've been to Ford's house a few times. It's new, or at least he's been working on it for a year or two. For the most part, he handles pick-up and drop-off, so I never have to drive here. When it comes to Connor, Ford does his best to make it easy for me.

Even though Ford gave me the security code for the gate to the cul-de-sac and for his front door, I still hesitate when my hand covers the handle of the front door. Maybe it's better if I press the doorbell.

This large modern lake house is as overbearing as the thought of the week ahead. At least I'll get to stare out onto the lake.

Lake Spark is a small town where people escape the city and enjoy boutiques and cute cafés. It's also the place where teenage Ford and I would escape to his family's lake house and get lost in time. I was seventeen when I first met Ford at a party on the lakeshore, and even though we lived in separate towns and he was in college, we made it work my senior year until the summer that changed our lives.

God, why does he want to live on this lake and be reminded of everything?

It's warm out, so I'm thankful I'm in a black tank top and jean shorts.

The door opens, and Ford greets me with a subtle grin. His white t-shirt and jeans draw me in because it only makes his eyes more intense. "Going to come in or wait for a pinecone or fox to get to you?"

As ridiculous as that sounds, it's completely accurate for Lake Spark. The woods surrounding the lake attract foxes, and apparently, his neighbor has had a few pinecones fall onto her head on a frequent basis.

"Sorry, just taking in my surroundings." He steps back, inviting me in with his arm. "The house looks good with the finishing touches, the outside, I mean." I take in all the changes as I enter his house, and I'm in pure amazement. "Inside too, it seems." Open-plan and everything state of the art.

"Thanks. The designer really picked up the vibe I was going for. Modern yet country, with a bit of local art thrown in. The pool is finished, and Connor loves that."

I keep stepping forward until I reach the floor-to-ceiling windows, and my eyes skip the view of the outside pool and head straight to where I can't tear my eyes away from the deep blue lake with glistening specks from the sunlight. "Beautiful," I say softly.

"Yeah… it is."

The way Ford's tone lingers in the air causes me to glance at him, and I see his eyes are on me, and I wonder if they ever left since I arrived. I don't say anything.

"Uhm, I can get your bags if you want and bring them to the guest room." He scratches his chin which has short stubble because he's a man now; he always was, but now he's older and still we're barely thirty.

"You don't need to do that. I'll get them in a minute."

He tips his head in the direction of the sliding doors. "Come on, the weather is far too great to be inside. Want a drink?"

"No, thank you." I follow him outside and again I'm caught by surprise.

The backyard is a bit more put together than the last time I was here. The pool isn't too big, but there is an inflatable alligator on the water. In the corner of my eye, I see a rope hanging from a willow tree that is an equal distance between the lake and the house. My eyes scan the scene, and I see the dock with a rowboat at the end of it, plus a small speed boat. The patio I'm standing on has new stone tiles and lounge furniture, with a bench swing which causes me to smile. I love bench swings.

"You did a really good job. Connor must love this." It's a lot more than my townhouse, but nothing has been a competition between us. Maybe internally, I've always known that Ford would be the cool dad with over-the-top presents, and I would be the mom with structure, and I'm okay with that. Ford and I don't speak negatively about one another, and I've never had a fear he would outshine me.

"I hope so. I guess we don't need to worry about him sneaking girls into the house or taking off with the boat yet. Give it a few years, though."

I huff a laugh. "If he is anything like his father then we are in serious trouble when he's a teenager."

"Nah, I know every possible hideout in a five-mile radius where he could sneak off to. Good luck to him," Ford proudly states as he tucks his hands into the back pockets of his jeans.

I walk to the bench swing and flop myself down, noticing

that Ford follows, sitting beside me. "This is such a difference from a few months ago when you were missing grass. It's now a real home."

He leans over with his elbows on his knees. "Happy you approve."

"You don't need my approval."

"Still, I like it."

Heat spreads through me at the way he says that, and it only intensifies because I can feel the warmth of his body next to me. I swallow some air and resilience.

"What time are we picking up the kiddo from camp?" I do my best to change the topic as I propel us to swing with my foot.

Ford chuckles under his breath, low, deep in his throat, and sinister. "This is where you're going to kill me."

My full attention whips in his direction. "What do you mean?" My foot brakes on the ground to stop the swing's movement.

"We have a slight change of plans." I can tell he is easing me into something.

I stand up and throw my hands to my hips. "Ford, what is going on?"

He looks up at me, with his smirk satisfied and strong. "Technically, when Connor is with me, then I make the parental choices."

"And?" I don't blink, and my tone must tell him that I'm not amused.

Ford slaps his hands on his knees before standing to tower over me. "He enjoyed camp last week, so I signed him up for another week."

"What?" I shriek, fuming.

"It's good for him."

"He's ten!"

"Exactly, which is why he wanted to do another week, and he will stay with Violet."

My jaw drops, and I swear I snarl. "You should have discussed this with me!"

"He is ten miles away. I visited hockey camp several times last week and will go this week to help out. He really wants this." Ford remains calm and collected.

I shake my head. "I can't believe this. How the hell is this supposed to be family time if Connor isn't even here?"

Ford says nothing, and instead crosses his arms and stares at the ground before he peers up at me with his smirk never fading. "Connor not being here is kind of the point."

"For what?" My voice cracks.

"Come on." Ford begins to walk toward the dock, and I trail behind, marching in pure rage, demanding answers.

"Calm down, Elle, we can use the next few days to talk and come up with a new schedule."

"Are you kidding me? I'm not staying here alone with you!"

I continue to follow him in tow as he grabs the rope from the dock post. "I think you are. Margo is expecting us tomorrow."

"You had this planned, didn't you? You could have called me, but you waited until I was here to tell me this change of plan." He is so unbelievable.

"Relax. You can still study for the Bar, enjoy the lake, wear that bikini you probably packed or no bikini at all, and at the end of the week, we can pick up Connor." Ford is completely satisfied with this situation as he calmly brings the rope to the rowboat.

My eyes dance between the boat and his hand holding the rope. "So now I'm going to be here for two weeks?" This week and another week with Connor.

"Oh, so you are staying then?" His smug look causes movement below my navel.

This is very bad.

Everything about this situation is a red flag. Ford and I have never been alone together overnight without Connor around. We always have safety blocks between us—our son, hockey games, and parent meetings. It's never been Ford and me alone in a gorgeous lake house, let alone the lake where we created a child.

I comb my hands through my hair and pull slightly as I pace a few steps back and forth, completely ready to scream.

"Who the hell does this? This is crazy."

He ignores me. "Are you joining me?" Ford holds up the rope in the air, and all he has to do is throw the rope in the boat and row off.

"Is this a joke?"

"No. Although I do hope you put sunblock on, it's a warm one out here." It's like he is oblivious to my rage.

Fuck me, he isn't flinching, he is completely in his winning mindset. I should march right back to my car and leave, but he's right. Margo is expecting us tomorrow, and I don't want to let her down, especially if she asked for me.

My heart races, and I debate what to say or do. My feet shuffle a step forward then back, but ultimately, an inner power beyond my train of thought makes me move to the rowboat.

Call it curiosity, but I'm too seething to drive anywhere anyhow, so I let my hand land in his warm offered palm to help me into the boat.

The moment I sit on the seat, I know this must be the shock kicking in for being tricked. No ounce of my normal intelligence would agree to this.

When Ford steps into the boat, causing it to wobble on

the water, I only watch as he sits down, slides his sunglasses on, and his muscled arms flex as he begins to row.

Do. Not. Stare. At his biceps. Just don't do it, Brielle.

I rip my eyes away from facing him and see water around us. How did I manage to get in a boat with him? It's like a curse was cast on me.

"Happy you decided to take a roll on my boat." He fails at suppressing his smile.

I fold my arms over my chest and sulk, refusing to speak.

"This is going to be a quiet ride if you aren't going to talk. But that's okay, I need you to listen anyway." He continues to row.

"I never get angry at you, but I might right now," I declare.

His lips quirk out. "Oh, I'm sure you will."

"And you seem happy about that."

He shrugs a shoulder. "You're cute when you're mad."

I nearly growl in aggravation. "Unbelievable. You have completely crossed a line."

"You have no idea." His cocky smirk doesn't fade.

So frustrating.

Ford slows down his rowing until we're floating. I look around to see we are far enough away from the dock that it would be a bit of a swim back.

"Why are we stopping?" I hear the caution in my voice.

"We're enjoying the view." His eyes don't leave me. "Want a water or something? I packed some drinks in the box over there."

I look over my shoulder and then do a double take when I see a little cooler. Shit, he really planned this.

"How considerate of you to trap me in this situation and provide beverages," I say, sarcastic. But *I am* a little parched, so I might as well enjoy a drink. I lean back and twist my body to reach for a water bottle from the cooler.

"No, considerate would be ensuring you can't escape so you can mull over something."

Turning around to face him, I drop the water bottle instantly as my body freezes.

Because Ford is leaning back against the bow, legs stretched out into the middle of the boat and one arm resting behind his head as he is lying in a relaxed pose, except that a small open velvet box is on display in his hand, with a ring sparkling in the sunlight.

"What is that?" I grind out.

"Your engagement ring, Elle."

Oh no.

This is not happening.

He is seriously doing it.

He's on a mission to break our promise.

FORD

10 YEARS AGO

The rain is drowning out the sound of Brielle's sobs as we sit in my car in a parking lot. Not being able to hear her sniffles doesn't offer any relief, though. Just looking at her and my heart breaks, and I already thought it shattered forty minutes ago when I picked her up.

My hand finds her soaked cheek, and I cradle her face, bringing her gaze to meet my eyes.

"I can't," she whispers again. "I can't do it."

I established that the moment I saw her this morning when she got in my car, and when I drove, I didn't push it, but I needed to hear her say it.

Now she has.

I nod once in understanding. "Then we don't. I promised you that the choice is yours."

"But…"

I wipe away a fresh tear with the pad of my thumb. "No buts," I assure her.

"They all think I'm not keeping the baby."

That's what our parents want. They gave us an ultimatum.

"Fuck what they think."

Her hand covers my own against her cheek. "It's not that easy."

Blowing out a breath, I know she's right. In this moment, I hate myself. It's my fault that she's eighteen and pregnant. She should be heading off to college; instead, she is dealing with this.

"I know." I sigh.

"I'm ruining our lives."

I react quickly to her statement. I bring my other hand to frame her face, and I hold her firm.

"Listen to me, you are not. We are in this together. Your decision is my decision. This isn't what we planned, not now, but it doesn't matter. You and I are now connected for life, and that ain't half bad." I'm barely hanging on but do my best to bring a positive.

Her eyes stay locked on me. "We're going to be parents," she laments.

"In around seven months, yes," I remind her, and the corner of my mouth attempts to smile, but I struggle and can't.

This is the girl I love, whose smile melts me more every time. It feels like yesterday I met her at a party on the lakeshore. Our families were in Lake Spark for the weekend, as they often are, since my family has a weekend house here. I met Brielle at a friend's party. She was wearing a light pink sweater that fell off her shoulder, and every time our eyes met, I was drawn to her a little more. Then, there around the bonfire, I made my move and asked her if she liked ice. She laughed in my face because she thought the next thing I would say is that I was a hockey player. She went hysterical and couldn't stop grinning when I, indeed, confirmed that I was in my first year of college playing hockey.

But our talk turned into hours. I gave her my hoodie by the end of the night, and over the weeks and months that followed, she was mine, and most weekends we would see one another. We could never keep our hands off each other, and every chance we had, we would lie on the shore late into the night or take the boat out to the secret lagoon.

I love her.

There isn't anything I wouldn't do for her. I see her in my future, watching my games, and one day, when I'm making millions, I'll give her anything she wants.

Right now, she wants this.

And I do too.

"We'll tell our parents together that we changed our minds," I breathe out.

I see the fear in her eyes.

For weeks, since the moment Brielle told me she thought she was pregnant and we took a test, we've been going back and forth over what to do. We told our parents together that Brielle was pregnant. They all made it clear what they thought the solution was, which is why we are sitting here in a parking lot for an appointment that we promised we would make.

As much as she's eighteen and I'm near twenty, we are barely adults.

I've been drafted for pro hockey, but I haven't signed a contract yet, and Elle is supposed to start college in a few weeks.

She sits back, causing my hands to drop from her face. She rests her head against the seat but turns to pin her eyes on me.

"Margo convinced them to let us have another option," I repeat the facts.

Margo heard our parents yelling in the living room after a summer BBQ where we thought was the opportunity to tell them. Brielle's parents were angry that I ruined their daughter's future of becoming a lawyer, reminding my parents that their only child is barely eighteen, and my father was worried my future as a pro athlete would be no more and that my girlfriend is ruining my focus on the sport, not to mention the example I'm setting for my little sister. My mother didn't have much opinion since we barely see her after my parents divorced.

Margo calmed everyone down and convinced them to be more supportive, but our parents' version of supportive is meeting us only halfway.

And this is where I try to suppress my own tears.

Because our other option should be easy, but it's not, as it means I don't have Brielle.

"There must be another way." Her voice cracks.

I interlace our fingers on the middle console of my car, and my eyes can't glance away from her fingers. In my world, I would ask her to marry me.

I swallow, knowing if I want to support her right now that I have to be the logical one. "I think we know it's the only way, Elle."

Already, I feel the pain in my throat from saying those words. She continues to cry, but I have to highlight the obvious. "You'll still go to college but will have time if you need it, your parents will help raise the baby."

"You'll go pro in hockey as planned."

"Yeah... and we won't be together."

Because that's the deal.

Her parents will still pay for her college, and my parents

will help to financially support the baby until I sign a contract, as long as Brielle and I follow our plans and aren't a distraction to one another. They don't want us in a relationship because they think we are dealing with enough, and our boundaries should be clear.

I wanted to scream that they could all forget it, but I'm not yet a star player who can give us the financial means, and I won't let Brielle give up on her dream of becoming a lawyer. I'll be so busy with hockey training and games for half the year, and I know it's not just financial, she needs help with raising the baby and support that I can't give when I'm on the road, but her parents can.

"It's for the best. We get to make something of ourselves instead of struggling with a newborn. It's a long road to becoming a lawyer, and I won't let you miss the opportunity to follow that path."

She nods in understanding.

The sound of the rain is somewhat calming at this moment.

"You can focus on your career. You're destined to be MVP. I guess you wouldn't be around much anyways for a relationship, plus balancing a child. It's probably for the best that we do this." I only half believe the words she just said.

"You know that's bullshit, although slightly practical." I scoff a sound. "Maybe the plan can change one day."

"Ford," she says my name with pure reverence.

I lean into her, our foreheads touching because I need her close. "A hockey career is only so long. Maybe when you finish college and I—"

She interrupts by slamming her long finger against my lips. "Don't. We'll drive ourselves crazy wondering if or when we might have a chance to be together again. I'll go crazy with that in the back of my head. You will too."

I kiss her finger away. "I want to believe there is more for us."

"Me too. But we have a child to think about, and we can't play around with trying to maybe work somewhere along the road. That's not fair to him or her. It would be confusing for all of us."

I can't even argue with that. "We'll both accomplish everything we wanted before we got pregnant. Even if this feels so wrong, yet I know it's right." I despise this, I'll never forget this moment.

"We're not being selfish, I guess that's what parents are supposed to do. We are putting this baby first. Our focus is trying to balance the baby and the career paths that will ensure they have a good future."

Our foreheads connect again, and I can taste a salty tear from her skin when I nip her nose with my lips. "It may be co-parenting and careers now, but we'll show them, Elle, and one day we can have it all."

"I can't think like that. My heart is already breaking, and I can't do this with the thought that maybe one day you will fix it. I'm protecting my heart. I need to be strong for this baby."

She's right. It's not fair to either of us to always be wondering. It's better to have no blurred lines on our plan forward. We have a kid to think about.

Brielle glances out the window then back to me. Her piercing gaze has me concerned because it strikes me in my heart. "I need you to know that I love you. That I want you involved with this little girl or boy's life. You'll be a great dad. But I think for both of our sanities, we accept that our only option is this, being apart." Her voice cracks. "Waiting for a moment when maybe we have a chance to make this work for the three of us will be painful, and that's not healthy for us."

I sink into the driver's seat. "We'll do this as two people who are putting our child first." I turn my key to start the car. "Let's go for a drive, we need some time before we talk to our parents."

She buckles her belt, and I get us on the road. A cruel twist of fate, the Verve Pipe's "The Freshman" comes on the radio, which is only fitting in this moment.

I'm at a total loss for what to feel right now. We're going to have a baby that I'm thankful for, but I wish the circumstances were more giving for us all.

We drive in silence for what feels like hours, but it's been maybe thirty minutes when I pull off the side of the road before a forest preserve.

Turning the engine off, I know exactly what to do right now at least.

"Come on, let's go to the back of the car."

She doesn't question me. We both get out of the car and get into the back. I bring her to my chest to hold, kissing her forehead. She wraps her arms around my middle, squeezing tight.

"I love you, Elle. Always will," I whisper.

"I do too, which is why this is hard." She glances up at me, and we kiss softly.

This is our last hour together like this, and we know it.

"I need you to promise me that we will put the baby first. Our hearts know the deal, and we accept that. It's the only way we can move forward with this. We eliminate the what-ifs and do exactly what this baby needs. Can we promise that?" she pleads softly.

I'm beginning to feel that her fear of a broken heart runs deeper than I ever imagined, and she has no idea my heart broke already an hour ago. Even if I have no intention of letting her go, right now she needs me to be the strong one.

She probably barely slept last night, and her body is changing. Hell, it's her life that is about to be upended more than mine. I get my hockey career, and she will be delivering a baby when she should be at a lecture. I have to do right by her. If she wants me to promise, then I have no other option, it's the best way to support her.

And if I'm being honest with myself, I would go insane waiting for us. Doesn't mean the idea of a different path won't be lingering inside me somewhere.

She looks exhausted, and with her face puffy from her crying, her eyes are so innocent and vulnerable. I kiss her forehead, nose, cheek, jaw, before placing a firm kiss against her mouth.

"I promise," I murmur against her lips, and she sighs with what might be relief, sinking deeper into my arms.

A man can tell a lie if his intentions are pure, right?

5

FORD

I've never forgotten that day. I'm sure we both think about it at some point between waking up and falling asleep, and here we are ten years later.

I can tell she wants to kill me. But she won't. Brielle is the type of woman who makes you pull over to save a squirrel. Except, right now? Well, she may just flip.

Her eyes don't tear away from the ring in the box that I'm holding in my hand.

This is unconventional, I know, but the opportunity has arisen.

"What the hell, Ford? Why is there a ring in your hand?" She quickly looks around the quiet lake, then her sight lands back on the ring before darting up to meet my eyes which are dead serious. "Unbelievable," she whispers. "You trapped me in the middle of the lake so I can't escape."

"Maybe." I smirk. "Get comfortable, we need to talk."

I've been thinking about how I want this all to play out since I saw her the other week. Hell, this whole situation has been years in the making.

My feelings for her have always been constant, and I've

done my best to keep the promise I made to her, but now I've hit my breaking point, and I'm not going to let us keep simmering under the surface.

"The r-ring, why?" she stammers softly.

I sit up and close the box then toss it between my palms, examining it. "Okay, so here's the deal. Tomorrow Margo is expecting us, and she might be under the impression that you and are back together—"

"What?" she nearly spits out.

My shoulder slants up toward my ear. "She hasn't been feeling her best lately, and she's anxious about her move," I remind her.

"I know, that's why I promised to see her, but how does this—" she motions between us "—come into play."

"She mentioned on the phone that she always wished to see us together and hoped it would be soon." It's the plain truth.

Brielle hums a sound before leaning back on the boat to get more comfortable on the slab of a seat. "Sounds like something she would say." A gentle smile of fondness displays on her lips. "She always sends me a Christmas card, not so subtly mentioning how Connor is the perfect image of two parents' love." She looks up at me. "But how does a ring come into it?"

I inhale a deep breath because maybe she will find this humorous... or not. "She told me her birthday wish, and it blurted out of my mouth that she didn't need to wait."

Brielle's beautiful mouth gapes open. "You lied to her?"

"Is it a lie? It will make her happy."

She runs her fingers through her hair. "Ford, you realize by lunchtime everyone else will think we are back together, and that eventually affects Connor."

I have thought every scenario through. How would I not?

Through the years, I've created a whole damn playbook of how our situation could go.

"She only really talks to Violet these days, and I'm sure my sister would get behind this to safeguard that Margo has an easy few weeks ahead. Connor wouldn't find out." Because by the time he does, then stage two of my plan will be in effect.

Brielle shakes her head slightly. "And let me guess, you didn't just lie that we are back together, you upped it and said we're engaged?"

Now I have to grin. "You know me so well."

She huffs out a breath and crosses her arms over her chest, and she pretends to be furious, but after a few seconds, the faintest of entertained smiles forms on her mouth that she desperately tries to suppress.

But only for a second, as disapproval returns to her look.

"I don't know, Ford. This is… not wise."

I lean forward to scoop up her hand and hold it between my palms. The sudden contact startles her, mostly because it's an electric shock between us, a current still strong, maybe more intense as time goes on.

"Margo is like a grandmother to me, always on our side, and when she told me on the phone that she really had hoped to see us back together before her time comes, because yeah, she got a little dramatic on the age front, then it just seemed like the right thing to do." It's the truth, although it's only the tip of the iceberg for what I have planned.

Brielle licks her lips, debating. "I know where you're coming from, I just…"

I duck my head down, then I peer up to catch her sight. "Don't trust us faking it for a day?"

Her lips roll in, and she doesn't answer, but her eyes say enough. She doesn't trust us.

"You know what I think?" I prod.

"What?"

"We've been able to avoid the obvious for years because we had things to keep us on a path. My hockey career, your education, Connor... but now hockey is no longer a factor, and you finished college and law school." I notice her chest moving up and down, and I wonder if she knows what's coming. "It's our time to re-evaluate."

She is quick to sit back, her hands falling out of my grasp. "Don't! Don't do this. You promised." She's enraged.

My body stiffens and shoulders straighten because it's time to lay down some hard truths as the sun warms us and the water glistens around us.

"We both are exactly where we started." Wanting each other.

She shakes her head, wishing not to listen, but damn, I know she believes in what I'm saying.

Energy shoots to my heart. I know relief is coming because I'm sharing it all. "We are still waiting. Fuck, we tried over the years to move on. Kept ourselves busy, we tried to find other people, and it always failed because it's not us, and Christ, the number of times I wanted to kiss you. This isn't new, you're thinking this too."

"Ford, it's true, hockey and becoming a lawyer are no longer our blockers, but we still have Connor to think about. I would hate myself if you and I were to try and it didn't work out, he would be crushed."

I stand up in a flash with a bitter laugh. "Do you really think we wouldn't work out? Are you crazy?"

She points a finger at me, rising from her seat. "Are *you*? You are the one who brought me to the middle of a lake to have this talk."

My hands come out to my sides, and I have a cheeky smile. "It's a great play. We're talking."

"On the lake where we probably conceived our son," she shrieks.

I hook my finger and nudge her cheek, purely entertained with her comment. "Ah, so that memory has flashed in your mind while we're out here."

She gives me a death glare and wags her finger at me. "Don't even." Her nostrils flare, and she wraps her arms around her body. Our eyes dance as we watch each other, standing in a rowboat on the lake.

Here is my chance. I'm throwing it all out there. "Stay the week with me and let's be everything we wanted, give us this. One week, and then you can keep the ring or say we fulfilled our curiosity."

Her jaw drops, and she moves to slam her hands against my chest, but she rocks the boat in the process. We both wobble, and I fall back to sitting against my propped hands, with my legs splayed out.

"Whoa!" She loses her balance, and her body lands right on top of me.

I have to smirk at fate giving us a hand. "See? Already in my arms."

Brielle doesn't move; instead, her nose tips up, and our mouths are dangerously close. I feel the magnetic connection between our bodies. It's taking willpower beyond my known ability not to slam my lips onto hers.

I rake my fingers through her hair to cradle the back of her head. "Think about it, but I know you already feel your answer. I see it in your eyes, and I feel your heart racing."

There is a glint in her eyes, they've already given me the answer I want to know. But my ears are waiting for her words.

She digs her fingers into the front of my t-shirt, and lucky me, her leg willingly adjusts so it's hooked over my thigh.

It's so perfectly clear to me. I've never seen her in a different light because she's always been mine.

"Ford," she pleads. "We are playing with fire."

"I'd burn the earth down if it means we get a chance." It comes out simply as my eyes stay fixed on her mouth.

I lean in to nuzzle my nose into her hair that smells of papaya.

"Row us back, Ford."

"You haven't answered."

"I can't think when we're like this," she says honestly.

"Because your body knows what it wants."

She moves to return to sitting on her spot. She's either burning from the sun or blushing, and I choose to go with the second option.

Brielle straightens her hair and avoids looking at me. "Row us back, please. I really need some space right now."

Blowing out a breath, I grab the oars. "Only if you promise not to get in your car and leave."

"I won't. Either way, I promised to see Margo tomorrow."

I begin to row and internally remind myself that I was voted MVP for four seasons straight because I'm always determined to win. And Brielle Dawson? She's the only goal I've ever wanted.

———

BRIELLE IS quick to march along the dock straight into the house. I let her go because I know when not to press.

Tying the boat up, I notice in the corner of my eye my neighbors Hudson and Spencer. Hudson is in his forties, looks like he drinks age-defying water, and is the head football coach for the Chicago Winds, and Spencer is home for a quick break from his baseball season because he has grand plans for his girlfriend.

I wave to them and meet them halfway at the point where the dock ends. Hudson has his baby girl Grace in a carrier, and she's staring at me, arms and legs out like a starfish.

Spencer is quick to pat my shoulder. "Hey, man, Brielle is here?" he asks.

"Yeah."

"I thought Connor was at camp," Hudson asks.

Spencer chuckles humorously. "He is. But Ford here has a scheme he's playing out."

Hudson looks between us. "Do explain."

I rub a hand across my jaw. "Brielle is staying here… we are working out a few things."

"Really? That's great." Hudson is enthusiastic.

Spencer gives him a blank look. "He tricked her into coming here, letting her think Connor would be here."

Hudson shoots his gaze to me. "Ooh, that's… not good?" It sounds like he doubts what he should think.

In this moment, I think I regret telling Spencer my initial plan the other day. Coincidentally, we went ring shopping together. While I was initially there to help him pick a ring for his girlfriend April, I might have picked one out myself that he doesn't know about.

"Ready for your big night?" I change the subject.

Spencer grins, ridiculously happy. "Completely. I got Hudson's approval."

Hudson throws an arm around Spencer. "He's going to marry my niece. He had to go through the checklist."

"She still needs to say yes," Spencer reminds Hudson.

"I doubt a no is coming your way," I assure Spencer. "Enjoy tonight." He has a big proposal planned.

Spencer tips his sunglasses down his nose to assess me. "Is there something you're not telling us?"

Hudson watches as he bounces the baby against his chest. "It's fine. I'm just…"

"Nervous your plan is going to fail?" Spencer finishes my sentence.

I tip my head side to side in contemplation. "Nah, we've been waiting for this."

Just then Brielle storms out my back door, breaking all our attention, and she stomps in her fast stride all the way to me, her face slightly fuming.

"Give me the box," she demands, holding out her palm.

I've never seen her so determined and buzzed with frustration, ridiculously sexy, and I also know not to deny her anything.

My hand fumbles into my pocket to pull out the box, and I quickly hand it to her. She grumbles and pivots so her back is to me.

She isn't fazed by my neighbors and friends since she has met them before. She's even worked for Hudson's sister at her legal firm. "Hi, Spencer. Hi, Hudson. Oh, Gracie is getting so big," she greets them before walking away like everything is dandy.

"Is that a yes?" I call out.

"I'm thinking," she yells back and disappears into the house.

It causes me to smile softly to myself in accomplishment.

"What the fuck? Was that an engagement ring box?" Spencer tries to grasp what just happened.

I bring a hand to the back of my head. "Yeah," I reply in a mesmerized tone.

"Uh, something you want to share?" Hudson asks.

"Nah, just upped the stakes a little. We're seeing Margo tomorrow, and she kind of thinks we're engaged."

"Let me guess, because you told her that," Spencer adds.

Hudson looks at me like I'm crazy. "What kind of neighbors do I live next to?"

"Don't worry, it won't be a fake engagement for long." I can't stop staring at my house where Brielle is inside probably pacing.

"Listen, as the older and wiser one of you two, let me offer some advice. It's only as complicated as you make it. Do yourselves a favor... don't make it complicated," Hudson lectures.

I glance at him as I cross my arms over my chest. "It's not complicated if we were always on a path back to one another."

"You have a kid." His tone is serious.

"And that's not the reason I want her, just a bonus," I admit out loud.

Spencer hisses a breath. "Ford, buddy, I am rooting for you both. I mean, it's obvious that you two are kind of hung up on each other. Just don't... I don't know... ruin an already good thing. You both co-parent so well. Now you're taking risks. You're taking a big chance here; don't pressure her or it could ruin everything."

I rub my face with my hands. "I've been patient long enough, and I finally have her here right here under my roof, alone time, me and her. I don't know how to do anything else right now."

"Yeah, I can tell. You look like a distressed retriever looking for his ball," Spencer informs me.

Hudson wobbles back and forth for the baby who is cooing and staring at me in wonder. "I get it, I really do. We've all been crazed by the women of our lives. There is no backing down, and I think you owe it to yourselves to figure it out."

"Thank you."

Spencer snorts a laugh. "I completely want status updates this week."

"I'm hoping to be too occupied for that."

Hudson chuckles at my reply. "By the looks of it from a few minutes ago, you may need to work a little extra hard. Brielle is in quite a state."

Rubbing the back of my neck, I smile tightly. "Oh, I know. But it just means she is contemplating." For some reason, I'm at ease; everything feels promising, or maybe I'm just optimistic.

But we are at the edge of our cliff, and I won't let us fall. Well, metaphorically, because figuratively I have every intention that we fall onto my mattress.

"Well, we'll let you head into your house of tension." Spencer waves two fingers in the air and begins to head off.

Hudson takes Gracie's little chubby arm and waves it in the air. "Good luck."

I wave them all off then take a moment to prepare myself. Blowing out a breath, I wonder for a second if I'm being selfish in this scenario.

I'm not. Because I'm only satisfied if Brielle is happy.

That means this plan can only go one way, which is why my feet move in the direction of the back door. I've always been supportive, gentle, and respectful of our dynamic.

But I'm throwing in the towel because persistence is key.

6

BRIELLE

B ack and forth.

That's all I have been doing for the past few minutes, tossing the small black box between my fingers.

Enraged is what I should feel. Ford tricked me and then dropped a bombshell proposition.

But, well, I'm not that furious. Or am I?

I stormed upstairs to one of the spare bedrooms. I'm growing slightly irritated that the designer did a good job, I can't deny that. This room is fresh with white, except for one accent wall of turquoise with matching throw pillows on the white bed.

I flop onto the mattress, blow out a long breath, and am thankful that Ford is outside with Hudson and Spencer, as it buys me time. I drop the ring box onto the mattress so I can pull out my phone which barely fits in my back pocket. Scrolling the screen, I hit Lena's name for a video call.

She picks up after two rings.

"Hey! How's the getaway?" She smiles, and it looks like

she's at her desk in her home office, as her hand seems busy with a computer mouse.

"Something has happened. Something bad. Like, *really* bad."

Lena sits up and abandons the mouse. "Is everyone okay? Connor?"

"Connor is fine. Probably having a great time. Long story short, but Connor isn't here."

"What?"

"Ford extended his camp for another week, and he is staying with his aunt. As much as I want to strangle Ford for doing that without consulting me, I know that Connor wanted to. Anyway, that is the least of our worries."

"How so? Ford completely made a parenting decision without you."

I shake off the notion. "It's Ford, he would never do anything he thought wasn't in Connor's interests, and besides, the camp is run by Ford's team, and he helps out, so he can check in on Connor a few times this week."

"You are far more chill than I would be."

"That would be because it's only the icing on the cake." I hold up my finger to pause her while Lena looks at me in anticipation. "Ford wants me to stay here this week… to… *reevaluate* our situation."

Her eyes grow big. "Didn't see that coming." She brings her fingers to her chin in contemplation. "Or did I? Hmmm… yeah, saw it coming." Lena grabs her water bottle for a drink.

"He got me an engagement ring."

She spits out her water. "Huh?"

I have to smile to myself because it's such a Ford thing to do, go a step too far if he knows it will make me smile. "I mean, it's kind of for pretend. He just wants to make Margo happy." Except I saw the conviction in Ford's eyes, and the ring feels like part of his long game.

"Okay, so what are you doing then? I mean, why didn't you get back in your car and drive back to Hollows?"

"I promised I would see Margo tomorrow."

"And tonight you will just…" She draws it out.

I sigh and roll to my back. "That's the problem. I'm under the same roof as Ford, and he threw one hell of an offer at me. I've been programmed to ignore whatever we left behind, but…"

A sly smile forms on Lena's mouth. "Brielle, I don't think you ever left behind the connection between you and Ford."

"Doesn't mean I should jump into bed with him."

"Is that what he's expecting?"

"I mean, he didn't say it as such, but I just kind of—"

Lena interrupts. "Assumed, because your subconscious has a fantasy it wants to play out."

I flop like a pancake to my stomach and attempt to defend my thoughts. "Do not judge me for noticing he has aged well. I mean, he literally has women throwing themselves at him, I would be blind to pretend otherwise."

She chuckles at me. "It's okay."

"No, it's not. What if we crash and burn again? It's taken ten years to get over him."

"You never got over him," she corrects me.

Lena is keeping me in check, damn it.

"This isn't some guy who I lost my virginity to and then see him again at a high school reunion. It's Ford. He's the father of our child, the man I see on a regular basis."

"He could also be the man whom you are missing an opportunity with."

I snort a sound because that's the joke of life on me. "I

think that's what scares me the most. What if it's everything I imagined and then some? It'll be a reminder that for the last ten years I didn't have that."

Lena clicks her tongue and smacks her lips out then back. "Good thing we don't go back in time then, we go forward."

I think for a few seconds. "Maybe. Anyhow, I should go. I have to deal with this." I hold up the ring box.

"You're going to wear it?"

"Haven't even opened the box, only stared at it."

"Keep me posted, but I am going to assume if I need to send you a letter that your address is in Lake Spark for the coming week, perhaps eternity." She flashes her eyes at me.

I don't answer, and we say goodbye.

Tossing the box onto the bed, I decide I can't hide in here forever. Walking out of the room and into the hall, the corner of my mouth curls up when I see Connor's room.

Walking to the door of his bedroom, I stand in awe. It's not over the top, nor too childish. There is a double bed with a navy-blue duvet, hockey sticks are hanging on the wall, and there is a desk with a globe and shelf of books. I know there isn't a game system here, partly because Ford and I agreed on no games or computers in Connor's bedroom, and also, I *know* Ford wants the game console in the living room because he loves to play just as much as Connor.

Most of all, I notice that this room is perfect because Connor is no longer a little child. Soon he will be heading into pre-teen life, then worse, the teenage years. It also means he is more aware, and we can talk in a more transparent way with our son. Ah hell, Connor would be on to Ford and me in a heartbeat, even if he doesn't tell us.

And I can't figure out if that's a positive or negative. Better yet, why am I contemplating Ford's offer?

"You approve?" Ford's voice startles me. His hands settle

on my shoulders to assure me that all is okay, or at least in this room. Everything else is still a toss-up. "Sorry, didn't mean to scare you."

I slowly turn and come face to face with Ford. "It's okay, just admiring the room. You really made it a home."

"Thanks. Ten is a hard age to decorate for. I'm lucky I hired a designer."

I nod once, unsure why I'm now calm when not long ago my body was riled. Now I'm just warm and overwhelmed because his eyes are on me, dipping down to stare at my mouth. I step back into the hall to get us out of Connor's room; I don't want to taint his space with the discussion that's about to happen.

But no words come out of my mouth. Instead, I stand there with my hands in my back pockets, and I try to avoid staring into Ford's eyes.

"Have you thought about it?"

Quickly, I glance up and then back down. "There is nothing to think about. It's ridiculous."

I do my best to escape, and I head straight for the stairs, but Ford grabs my arm so I don't get far. In fact, I'm now closer.

To him.

His breath.

His scent.

Those eyes that hold me every single time.

"It's not. Elle, we've been doing a damn good job with keeping our promise, but only on the surface."

My eyes shoot up to lock with his because he pretty much nailed down my theory too.

"It doesn't mean that we should have a week of fun to bury our curiosity."

Ford is quick to step forward. Our mouths are now inches

apart, and he hasn't let my arm go. "I'm not talking about fun. This is a little more. We have some truths to tell and lost time to make up for. Fun is what you do when there's no history, no future. You and I already have half of that."

"We also have parenting together."

"And we're more than just parents. We deserve more," he is quick to counter. I shake my head gently, and Ford hooks his finger under my chin, guiding my gaze to him. "Let me prove to you that we can have it all. It's our time."

"No pressure or anything," I retort.

It earns me a grin from Ford. "I've already taken the step to possibly make this fucking awkward between us because I've made it clear what I want to try. So you might as well make the leap."

"It's a big leap." I stare blankly at him, wondering why my body still feels so incredibly comfortable in this situation.

"I don't do small for *anything*." The innuendo is there, and I snort a laugh.

He nuzzles his nose against mine as he lets my arm go and instead opts to rest his hand on my waist.

"Oh, I know. You got a ring," I reply.

"Which you haven't given back. You're considering this week." His voice goes soft and raspy.

"So many thoughts are floating in my head. How convenient is the timing, huh? Only when we both seem to have gotten what we wanted."

"It's not like I'm bored and thought 'oh let me fuck up my co-parenting arrangement with the only woman I ever want to share kids with.' It's that I know you've almost achieved your goals and my career is over. Everything that caused that promise is no longer a trigger for us to pretend that we were able to move on."

We are one and the same. His words could literally fall off my tongue except I'm not brave enough to speak them. Lucky for us, Ford woke up determined today.

I lean my head to the side, attempting to get an extra inch or two between us, although the damage has already been done. I'm completely affected by this man.

On second thought, I slant my head back to him and bring my palms to his face, as if I'm going to be bold and kiss him.

He's here for it, as his hand on my side yanks me tightly to his body.

My heart races because I've played this scene in my head a million times. I've imagined what it would be like, I've secretly hoped for it.

I trace his stubbled jawline with my lips, merely a touch but enough to get the oxytocin from this man that I think my body may need to survive. It's why I always allow the gentle touch here or there from Ford.

Closer.

So close.

Nearly the end.

But the moment our lips brush, the feeling is too intense.

I step back, aware that crossing the line with Ford will be a flame that was dimmed but now will be rekindled.

"I think tonight I'm going to take it easy. Study a bit for the Bar."

Even avoiding looking at him, I know he's disappointed. "I can throw some steaks on the grill or order a pizza."

I swallow the chance that I let slip away. "I'm not that hungry."

"Okay. Well..."

"I'll see you in the morning for Margo's."

"Will you play along for Margo?"

I touch my hair nervously. "I'll sleep on it."

Ford throws his hands up in surrender. "That's all I can ask. If you need anything, then just find me. My bedroom door will be open."

My eyes gawk at him in a double take.

He quickly pinches my cheek on the way by. "Take that how you want. All options are on the table, but just remember, I don't sleep with a shirt on," he calls out in passing.

———

AFTER ATTEMPTING TO STUDY, exchanging some texts with my son, and changing into pajamas before braiding my hair, I tried to sleep. An epic fail, as I tossed and turned for a good hour.

It's the middle of the night when I venture downstairs for a drink. The kitchen is big and should be filled with family meals and kids. I shake my head when I catch myself daydreaming. I'm relieved to find myself alone in the kitchen.

Yet disappointed at the same time.

By the time I'm back upstairs, I slow my steps in the hallway, well aware that Ford's bedroom is a magnetic pull, and he wasn't lying about keeping the door open.

I can't help myself, and I stop to check out the view of Ford sleeping. He's a stomach sleeper, so I only see his bare back under the stream of light from the hallway. He looks peaceful. At least one of us can sleep tonight.

God, I could watch him like this for hours. After I had Connor, I did a few times. Sometimes when Connor was a baby and would sleep on Ford's chest, and another time quite recently. Except, I don't think Ford knows. He was resting in the hospital after a game where he yet again got hit too hard.

I won't go down memory lane, I repeat to myself.

I step to the side but don't get far.

"You know you can come under my covers, and I promise to be a gentleman," Ford speaks in a drowsy tone.

I roll my eyes, amused, and walk into his room. "Pretending to sleep?" I plant my hands on my hips.

Ford rolls to his back and slides up the bed against the backboard.

Holy hell, this view is weakening any shred of resolve between my legs.

His biceps are just ridiculously toned but not too bulky, and bare-chest Ford is always a winner too.

He holds open his duvet. "Come on, it's cold."

"It's summer."

"And you're cold." His eyes drop down to my chest, and I look to realize my nipples are hard underneath my tank top. I bring my arms up to cover myself. "I promise," he insists.

I step forward, hesitate, then take another step before easily walking to his bed and sliding under the covers. I don't recognize my willingness right now, but I don't question it either.

We lie on our sides and face one another, oddly aware that this isn't sexual but is by no means platonic either.

"I couldn't sleep," I confess.

His face softens. "You still braid your hair at night."

I look at him peculiarly. "You remember?"

"Every detail. Why were you watching me?"

"I don't know. I was remembering when you were in the hospital a year ago."

Ford slides my braid over my shoulder. "I'm beginning to think watching me when I sleep is a habit for you."

"Ah, so you knew I was there?"

"The hospital? Yeah, a nurse told me."

"How come you never let me know?" I snuggle into the mattress, apparently feeling like I'm going to stay here.

Ford takes it as his cue to also get more comfortable in bed. "Because I wouldn't have let it go, so I kept my mouth shut."

"Until now." My voice sounds delicate.

"There are many times we could have openly questioned ourselves, but we didn't. Here we are now, tired, in my bed and with opportunity."

I playfully swat his shoulder.

"I meant this week, not in this moment. Although, I do have you in a prime location right now." Ford pretends to consider.

"Go to sleep."

"You're staying here?"

I shrug a shoulder. "I'm cold," I remind him.

"Then come here."

He brings an arm around me, encircling us together. When he kisses the top of my head, I can't help but feel like we never missed a page, because lying with him in bed feels as natural as the air I breathe.

"You have good arms," I comment.

"I'm not even going to give a comeback because you know you just gave away that you've been checking me out."

"You're the father of our child, I'm always checking you out," I declare matter-of-factly.

He squeezes me tighter. "I'm more than that and you know it."

I don't answer, instead opting for us to lie with each other, occasionally glancing and touching one another's face or an arm or tracing a vein from the top of a hand up.

Staying in his bed is a one-way ticket to confusion.

"Night, Ford," I whisper.

He sighs as I begin to wiggle out of his bed. "Your loss."

"I'm sure," I retort.

Walking out of his room, I know that the last few hours are enough to encourage me to jump over the cliff.

Because the next morning when I wake, I pick up the ring box.

7

FORD

Staring into my mug of coffee as I lean against the open sliding door to outside, I might appear calm, but I'd be lying if I said that I wasn't nervous. Throwing my shirt on hasn't been a priority this morning either.

I haven't seen Brielle since last night when she walked out of my bedroom after giving me a tease of getting her warm in my bed. She doesn't even know that's what she was doing, or if she did, then she played it steady. Needless to say, I didn't get back to sleep easily, especially as the smell of her hair remained on the pillow.

Damn papaya.

It's almost nine. We are due to see Margo in an hour. It won't take long to drive to her home. Margo runs a routine, and by ten she wants morning tea in her garden, or the conservatory when the weather is too cold.

I tap my finger on the mug handle, and I decide that I'm not in much of a mood for caffeine. I walk out onto the patio and set the cup on a table, heading straight for the edge of the tiles to look out and study the middle of the lake. Old man Pete is swimming. He does it without fail as long as there's no ice. Geez, I hope I'm capable of that when I'm his age.

The pattering of heels grabs my attention, and I twist my body to glance over my shoulder.

Fuck me, Brielle is stunning. Her hair is down in waves framing her face, and her shoes are open-toed to show the pale blue polish that matches her fingernails. She had to choose a baby-pink near-white dress? It's exquisite, with short sleeves, yet it flows out at the waist to above her knees. I never had a fifties-housewife fantasy in my head, but my mind is spinning.

The sunlight shines on her as she stands still by the sliding door. "Really? No shirt? I should have known. Anyway, we should be going soon; I want to stop and pick up some fresh flowers for Margo."

I smirk, kind of proud of my unintentional shirt move, before I scrub a hand across my jawline, taking a breath to prepare myself for the obstacle of the next few hours— keeping my body in check.

I slide my hand into my dark jeans pocket. I'll throw on a white buttoned-down t-shirt. Margo likes effort.

"Yeah, sure. Don't you want some breakfast?"

Elle giggles. "You know she is going to have an array of tea sandwiches and cake that we can't say no to, right?"

I grin to myself. "That she will." I walk in Brielle's direction, and when I notice her adjust her earring, I'm blinded by the light of a diamond on her finger.

A victorious smirk comes over me, and I clear my throat to play this cool. "Nice ring."

She holds her hand up to examine it. "Not bad. Some guy lost his mind and decided to spend God knows what on this so I can wear it for a few hours." She gives me a pointed look. "Only a few hours," she warns.

I chuckle under my breath as I slowly stride to her. "Whatever you say."

She points her finger at me. "No tricks, Ford."

"I wouldn't dare," I lie.

Brielle pouts a sound before pivoting to head in the direction of the garage.

Step by step.

That's how I will get her.

————

AFTER DRIVING into town in silence, I parked on Main Street so we could run into the florist. An overpriced bouquet of purple blooms later, we are walking down the sidewalk, and I'm carrying the flowers that I'm sure will soon make me sneeze.

Brielle touches my elbow to grab my attention. "There's Piper."

My eyes follow her line of sight, and I indeed see Piper holding baby Gracie as she closes the car door. Piper is married to Hudson, so she's my neighbor too.

"Hey, Piper," I call out.

She immediately looks up and smiles. "Hey, Ford." She looks confused when she notices who is at my side. "Hey, Brielle, I didn't know you would be here in Lake Spark this week, with Connor still at camp."

Brielle gives me the side-eye. "Well, it seems everyone knew Connor would still be at camp except me."

I can only give my temporary fake fiancée an innocent look.

"Oh." Piper looks between us. "Will you two stop at April and Spencer's later? He popped the big question last night, so we all, of course, need the play-by-play."

"We'll try," I say.

Gracie fusses, and Piper bounces the near toddler against her hip. "This one has been keeping us busy. No rest for the wicked, right? I'm hoping the drugstore has something for her skin."

"What's wrong?" Brielle asks, concerned, and reaches out for Gracie's little finger.

"She has a little eczema, and nothing seems to work."

"Try pure chamomile oil. There is also this oat oil for the bath. It's supposed to be for Chickenpox, but it works wonders in general. Connor had the same problem at Gracie's age, kept me up for hours some nights because he was itchy," Brielle explains as Gracie grips her fingers.

Piper seems grateful for the advice. "I will go grab those items right now."

They're both chatting about something, but I zone out. Mostly because guilt hits me. I missed a lot when Connor was a baby, and Brielle took the brunt of it all. The sleepless nights, teething, every fever and cold. Her mom helped, but I should have been there.

After we say our goodbyes, we walk to my car and get in, the flowers finding a home on the back seat of my Ferrari.

I start the engine but freeze, debating if I should bring this up now, but the thought wrestles in my brain. "You don't resent me, right?" It falls off my tongue. My gaze leads me to Brielle who looks at me, unsure.

"What do you mean?"

"When Connor was a baby, you had it a hell of a lot harder than I did."

"Did I?" I can't read her.

I touch the top of her hands that are folded on her lap. "Don't pretend. We both know you did."

She sighs. "It's all a blur of sleepless nights. It doesn't matter. You are a great dad," she assures me.

"That's not what I'm asking. You can be a great dad but miss moments. I wasn't there enough for you."

Her eyes narrow in on me. "What do you want to hear? Yeah, it was tough. But you had hockey and…"

"It's okay, be honest."

"I don't want to say it's resentment or disappointment. You were building a career that provides for our son. I just… I don't know…" She rolls her shoulder back. "Let's just go to Margo's, we can't be late."

"Don't change the subject." I hear the edge in my voice.

"Okay, yes. Sometimes I look back and hate how the cards fell, but I also don't regret it. We have a great boy, and it all worked out in the end." She avoids my eyes and looks out the window.

I laugh without humor. "I don't think it worked out."

"Stop saying that!" She raises her voice which surprises both of us. "I mean, Ford, I have a whole list of things that I wish were different, things I could be mad at you for, but we have to parent together, so I let it go."

"Tell me the list," I urge, with my eyes never blinking.

She shakes her head. "No."

"Yes."

"Fine. If you want to go down this road, then let me rip the band-aid off." Her voice is pure frustration. "I hate that it's my choice that put us in this situation."

My heart sinks, and I want to immediately comfort her. I urge her to turn her body in my direction by touching her arm. "Don't. I'm promising you that it's not your fault." Her eyes well with water, and now I feel like an ass for getting her into an emotional state. "I need to hear you say it, that you understand that I don't believe it's your fault. Tell me," I plead.

She nods once. "I do believe you."

"Go on. What else is on the list? Every little thing."

Her eyes flutter to keep her tears in. "You weren't there when Connor had Chickenpox, that was hell. Or when I had to cram for a midterm, but Connor wouldn't sleep, and my parents were on vacation. I hate that you got him a game console when he was only four."

"Whoa, it was educational," I say in an attempt to make her smile.

"It was a nuisance."

I touch her cheek and rub my thumb along her cheekbone. "What else?"

"How every time Connor and I would visit you at a hockey game, you made it a grand experience for him that he would talk about for weeks. Which is amazing, but I couldn't escape hearing your name more than usual. And God, that blonde you dated once was a real bitch, way too doll perfect."

"She didn't hold a candle to you, and I hated that nerd from your poli-sci class. Could have throttled him."

"I know. And he didn't even like pizza, what kind of person is that?" Now she is attempting to lighten the mood.

"I hate that I see you all the time. A great mom, so fucking sexy, and I wish every man knew that I have a claim to you."

"Caveman," she one-tones.

I twirl some of her hair around my finger. "I'd commit murder for you."

"Now you just sound like a true crime in the making."

A half-smile creeps on my lips. "My only crime is not confronting us sooner."

"We were occupied."

"Now we're not."

She laughs and licks her lips. "No, now you have me pretending to be your fiancée, and I have a Bar exam to cram for."

"Our parents will love it," I joke because they may all kill me. I think over time, Brielle's parents slowly disliked me more due to my career, and my own father still believes she's the distraction I don't need.

Brielle gives me a doubtful look. "I'm sure my father still has a shotgun somewhere."

We sit in my car in silence, unsure if this is relief or if the pot has been stirred even more.

"Come on, we really can't be late," she insists.

I nod and get to work on pulling us out of the parking spot.

———

WE ARRIVE at Margo's mansion, with her well-manicured plants and long driveway. She has help, but still, this feels a little too much considering she lives here alone.

Getting out of the car, I circle around the front to open the passenger's side. I offer my hand to Brielle, and she shakes her head, amused. I'm going to be over the top.

She's holding the flowers in one arm. "I swear to God, do not make me regret this."

"Come on, it's for a good cause."

Margo is sad to be moving but feels that Florida and assisted living is the right choice, as she has a son down there, plus the warm weather all year round will be beneficial to her.

We walk to the front door, my hand finding a permanent spot on Brielle's lower back. Someone who helps out around the house lets us in and sends us to the backyard.

Walking out and the fountain and plants are the backdrop for Margo, wearing her pearls, sitting at a table decked out in drinks and food.

She claps her hands together and stands. "Wonderful, you two are here."

I smile as we greet her with hugs.

"Of course, someone is getting younger here." Brielle offers Margo the flowers.

"Darling, age is just a number. Thank you, these are beautiful." Margo holds her hand out to the table. "Please sit, I had my chef prepare a few things."

I hold out Margo's chair, and when she's settled, I find my place sitting next to Brielle.

I'm quick to interlace our hands on the table. Brielle stiffens slightly, but I know she's trying to hide her smile because pushing her buttons is something I can't resist.

"I'm so happy to see you both before I move… and together. Miracles do happen," Margo gushes.

I lean in to kiss Brielle's cheek. "They do, don't they?" I lay it on thick.

Brielle tightens her grip on my hand; it's a tad on the tight side, but I'm just going to assume she's been working out.

"Was his proposal something special?" Margo questions.

My fiancée looks at me. "Yes, Ford, do tell."

"I would like to think so. Just us, I took Brielle to this lagoon that's hidden off the lake, and we had a picnic. It's a special place. When we were teenagers, we would go there, and it's also the place that we –"

My girl cuts right in. "Ford, I think that's enough details." She smiles tightly.

"Sounds delightful and look at that ring." Margo reaches

onto the table, and Brielle is quick to offer her a view of the ring. "Tasteful. A lot better than the original choice."

"Original choice?" Brielle asks, perplexed.

I have to divert us. "Wow, are those cucumber-and-cream-cheese sandwiches? You know the way to make me happy."

"Yes, dear, I also have those egg-salad-with-pickle sandwiches. I thought maybe Connor would be with you both, so had the chef make peanut butter and jelly too."

"Thoughtful. Connor is at camp this week. His father thought another week of camp would be a real treat for all of us." Brielle is laying it on heavy, while subtly letting me know her dissatisfaction as of late.

Margo indicates for me to pour her some tea. "Little boys have a lot of energy. I'm sure it's exactly what Connor needs."

"Exactly," I say as I fill her cup. "Brielle is about to sit the Bar," I proudly announce.

Margo looks at her with pure elation. "I knew you would get there."

"Well, I still need to pass it."

"You will," I promise her.

"What will you do after?" Margo wonders.

Brielle takes a sip of water. "The law practice where I had an internship and worked in paralegal part-time has a position opening up, so that's a start."

"But where will you two live then once you are married?"

Brielle and I both croak a sound. "It's in discussion. We have school for Connor to think about," Brielle answers. She isn't a great liar, but she's trying.

"There are excellent schools here," I state. "Plus, the house is all ready for Brielle. Her bench swing, favorite-colored pillows, and a home office. Then there is the lake that she loves more than she cares to admit."

Brielle's eyes snap to me because she knows I'm not pretending. The dots connect in her head. She was in my thoughts when I designed the house.

"Is Connor excited that his parents are back together? He must be over the moon." Margo takes a sip from her tea.

"I think he will be ecstatic at the wedding. A simple wedding, just the three of us." I have no idea what I'm spewing or why this comes so easily. Or why I'm speaking in the future tense, other than I'm manifesting some serious plans.

"You must send me a gift idea. Spare no expense."

Brielle laughs nervously. "Don't be silly. We don't need gifts."

"Fine. When the next child comes, then let me buy a gift."

I nearly choke on the coffee that I poured a minute ago.

"That will be a while. I'm still young and need to focus on my career. Have to mentally prepare for the three kids under our roof, probably all boys, and with Ford's personality too, so pure mischief." Brielle speaks without taking notice of me.

But now I'm wondering what her mind is spinning.

"Your parents?" Margo asks.

Brielle and I look at one another before I jump in and answer. "Best not to talk to them about this."

"Hmm, I can only imagine. You know, they will come around. They did last time, when it came to raising Connor. You just need to be firm."

"Were we not firm enough last time?" I'm slightly offended.

Margo looks between us all very seriously. "You were both young, in a delicate situation, and sometimes you need a little extra intervention. Your parents saw you both as their children, children they needed to guide, and they thought one way was the right way. I just stepped in to let them know there had to be a compromise on their path."

Brielle's eyes dip down to look at the patio floor.

I breathe out a breath and bring my arm around Brielle's shoulders. "We are grateful for that. Do you think there was another path that none of us explored?"

Margo seems taken aback. "Adoption, although a gift to many, wasn't what either of you wanted. Or do you mean marriage? Your ring could have been an option, but then I'm not sure either of you would be where you are today. Sometimes we get our true love later. Look at you two now, so many things to be proud of. A great son is one of them, and now you both get to have what you've been waiting for."

I rub warmth into Brielle's shoulder as we listen to Margo, and I'm grateful Brielle didn't question the ring remark more.

The next hour we talk about Lake Spark town gossip and roses. We would love to stay longer, but Margo needs rest.

As we wrap up our time together, Brielle and I stand. This time our hands connect of their own accord, my free hand sliding down her spine as she leans in to hug Margo.

"You look so healthy and happy," Margo notes to us.

"Thank you," Brielle says. "I'm glad to have seen you again."

"Me too, and I know Ford will treat you right, he's been waiting to be your husband for years."

Brielle laughs. "Why do you say that?"

"Before he upgraded your rock, he had a cheap little one when you two were kids, but you know this."

No, she did not.

Brielle freezes for a second or two before giving me a piercing gaze.

I ignore her for a moment. "I'll call you later in the week, Margo," I promise.

"Don't be silly. You two have a week to yourselves without Connor. Go wild and never leave your home." She winks at me.

I keep Brielle close as we walk to the car. I open the door for her, and she slides onto the seat, clearly agitated.

When I make it to the driver's seat, she is quick to slide the ring off her finger and hand it back to me. "Why does Margo think you got me a ring when we were younger?"

Yep, saw this coming about one minute ago.

My lips press together as I tuck the ring into my pocket, unsure what to say, but honesty is the best policy. "Because I did. Before the appointment, I thought it could be an option. But then Margo walked me through the reality of you not having your dreams, and the next day, when we decided to keep Connor, then something inside me thought our choice was right, so I returned the ring. We were young, confused, and none the wiser."

She sits there quietly for a second. "Why didn't you tell me?"

"Because I'm a selfish asshole who realized that you having support would be better, and you already looked like you were breaking." I heave a sigh.

"Drive back to the house, *now*." She's insistent, but I can't figure out if she's more mad or sad.

I know better than to push her to talk. Brielle is more open when you are patient and let her lead. This is why our car ride back is a stiff silence with an old Goo Goo Dolls album playing, but I make no mistake that I hear a sniffle or two as she stares out the window.

My veins are filled with remorse for how today is going.

I'm unraveling us.

Which up to now was hard to do, as we were tightly wound in what we thought was right.

I bite the inside of my cheek, trying to contain myself from saying anything else. The last thing I want is for her to break. Hell, I don't want her shedding any tears.

The road ahead is winding around the lake, it's dangerous if I'm not careful.

Much like us.

But I keep my hands on the steering wheel, in control.

As soon as we are back at the house, I park in the driveway, and she storms out of the car. I follow her at the speed of light. We both stop in the middle of my lawn, clearly about to face off.

"Ford Spears, why are you torturing us?"

8

BRIELLE

Ford is stirring so many emotions inside of me, more than average.

"I'm torturing you? Because of this morning?" he dares to ask, his hands hanging at his sides.

I throw my hands up in the air, completely helpless. "Tricking me, getting us alone, a ring. A ring, Ford? Who is their right mind does that? Then this morning, and I..." Didn't want to hear what deep down I knew he probably thought long ago.

My head falls in sorrow.

He steps forward, but I'm quick to hold my hands up to stop him. "Do not step closer to me," I warn.

His head dips down, and his sight tips up to grab my attention. "You feel it too."

"I need you to look away with your luscious puppy eyes because they will not make me fall into your arms."

A total lie.

He knows it too because he smirks. "We can't change the past, but we can write the future, and I'll be damned if it's anything except waking up to you."

My brow slides up. "You're so sure of us."

"Tell me I'm wrong. Tell me I'm imagining that you and I can't let go of one another. Just tell me and I'll give this up… but you can't."

"You didn't give me a chance to tell you." I tip my hip out with my hand on my waist.

He grins sheepishly. "Please, go ahead." He doesn't sound convinced.

"I…" Have no clue what I'm doing, that's what. I look up at him and my heart is fully his, and it scares me. Ford has the key, and I know he'll hide it so nobody will ever have it but him. "I'm so angry," I admit softly.

"I gathered." He doesn't seem fazed.

The lids of my eyes slowly close then open but no calm hits me. Instead, a hurricane passes over my heart and moves through my throat on full windspeed because everything rolls off my tongue in a wave.

"I can't tell you that you're wrong. Okay? Happy? Is that what you wanted to hear?" I raise my voice, my chest thumping with emotional fury. "I couldn't sleep last night because I'm stuck in this beautiful house on a lake that has some mystical powers to get me pregnant and engaged in the span of a decade. I laid awake last night on a soft mattress wishing that for one night I had the ability to let go and be in the moment. With you." Ford looks at me, mute, that I'm at last breaking. Our eyes lock in recognition. "Because yeah… you, Ford, I want more than anything, but we share a son who doesn't deserve a clusterfuck of epic proportions if we get this wrong."

We both seem taken aback by my little monologue.

But before either one of us can say something, a spray of hard cold water comes up from the grass. I shriek from the sudden surprise, my mouth gaping open as I try to understand. Instantly I'm getting soaked through, and the shock has me frozen as I take in what is happening.

I don't realize until Ford begins to laugh. It's only then that I connect that it's the sprinkler, and Ford by chance just missed the brunt of the water. I'm standing in front of him wet, and my dress is now a second skin.

"Are you kidding me?"

He tries to hide his laugh. "You're standing on the grass. It's on a timer."

"Is this my luck? What other stunts will happen on this property?" My hair is now soaked, and I wipe away water from eyes that probably have mascara running.

"You're cold."

"It's summer," I reply.

"And you're cold." Ford steps into the stream of water, and I realize he is repeating what we said last night because my nipples are clearly peaked, and his eyes have noticed.

"It's cold because you keep the air-conditioning high and get me trapped in sprinklers," I argue back, one-toned and unsure what is happening.

The sound of the water becomes a backdrop or it's my ears ringing as my heart beats fast. That's the reason the world seems to be going silent around us. Ford is now drenched in water and so very close, his eyes hungry.

"You're in the moment," he highlights. "With me."

A smile tugs on my lips, because this moment feels like relief and perfection rolled into one. The setting for a memory, and I know it will be one that I'll smile about for years to come.

Because before I can say anything, his hand grabs the back of my neck, and he pulls me to his mouth. His lips slam down onto mine, and I'm drowning not in the water but him. My hands are quick to frame his face in hopes of finding balance, and luckily, his arms snake around my middle to yank me tight to him.

Ford swallows my breath as our mouths realign. Kissing him sets off an explosion inside of me, yet I'm struggling to register it, with my body in slight shock because it remembers his lips.

Only when his tongue slips into my mouth do I relax. Even though I knew where he was all along, this kiss is my lost treasure that I finally found.

I moan into his mouth, which only encourages Ford to kiss me harder. I offer more by slanting my chin up. I can't get enough.

He holds me tighter and kisses me softer, then he growls as he brushes his lips along mine. "Finally," he speaks against the corner of my mouth before giving me a quick peck as a parting.

We need to breathe actual air.

Staring at one another, we're both panting and soaked. Ridiculous smiles are displayed on our faces, and I lean my forehead in so he can kiss my temple.

"I'm staying. This week, I mean," I confirm.

Ford blinks at me, with water running down his face. "I wouldn't have let you leave anyway, and you know we are more than a week."

I don't argue. "Kiss me again," I request.

At the speed of light, he fulfills my request, a kiss full of longing and hope. Tender yet firm because we are working against external forces, and water is as powerful as waiting ten years.

We stay this way for what feels like minutes until we break apart, and without warning, he throws me over his shoulder fireman style and walks us out of the sprinklers.

I giggle and admire his flexed muscles beneath wet

clothes that can carry me with ease. He twirls me around before he walks to the side yard.

"What are you doing?" I wonder.

"As much as making out with you on my lawn is a dream come true, we need to get out of these wet clothes."

My stomach flips, possibly with nerves, but mostly excitement. Today, nothing else matters except us.

Ford gets us to the back sliding door and walks us in until he plops me down in the hall by the stairs.

Then I'm on him again. This time I kiss him, short, fast, and over and over. He begins to unbutton his shirt, and I'm quick to assist, peeling the shirt off his arms until it's on the floor, our mouths never parting.

I hop onto him and wrap my legs around his waist before he takes the first step on the stairs. Halfway up, we fall to a step, and I straddle him as our tongues continue to fuse together.

Now that water is no longer working against us, I feel more. My body is more attuned to what is happening. I'm sensitive in all the right places, and Ford has the key to every single spot.

"We need to get you out of this." Ford's voice is a sexy raspy tone as he assesses me from the waist up and back down.

"Likewise," I counter, and my fingers begin to fumble with the belt of his jeans. The sound of the buckle loosening is mixed with our labored breaths as our lips run wild on our mouths and necks.

He uses his weight to lift us up, and we continue our journey upstairs. Ford walks us straight to his bedroom where he lays me down gently on his bed.

I bring my finger to my mouth to nibble as I watch Ford tower over me and step out of his pants.

Ford in dark boxer briefs and nothing else is a view I could stare out for hours, days, and years. I'm not into muscular overload on guys, but Ford is toned. I could take a marker—or my tongue—and trace every line.

A cocky smirk spreads on his mouth. "Better than the Ford in your fantasies?"

"Debating," I quip.

Slowly, he steps forward, his knees hitting the edge of the mattress. My feet plant on the duvet with my knees up. All he would have to do is lift the skirt of my dress and I'm his for the taking.

His eyes shoot me a warning; pure sin is on his mind.

I gasp slightly when he touches my knees, and he glides the pads of his fingers up my thighs. Every inch higher causes the ache between my legs to intensify.

Ford leans down to delicately kiss my inner knee. "So damn beautiful."

The feeling of my cheeks blushing doesn't faze me; I'm far too familiar that this man electrifies my body.

In a swift movement, he hooks his fingers under the waistband of my panties without moving my skirt up, and it wouldn't matter, as his eyes stay fixed on me. Ford yanks the wet material down my legs, and my feet move to slide them off easily. He throws the wet fabric to the side.

My heart races for what comes next.

Ford holds his finger up, indicating for me to wait a second.

"Now you want to wait?" I tease.

He ruefully shakes his head and walks to his closet on the side, leaving me splayed out on his bed. I can't see from my angle, but he disappears into the closet and remerges with clothes.

Coming to the bed, he throws a hoodie and boxers at me.

"We need to get you warm."

My jaw drops, completely shocked by this change. "W-what?" I stutter.

Ford crawls onto the bed and cages me underneath him. I hate when he has a look that informs the world that he won.

"Oh, trust me, I'm ready to break this mattress and rip every sheet in this house for the way we need to seal this reunion."

"Then what's the damn problem?" I'm stunned.

He leans down to breathe near my ear before placing a kiss in that sensitive spot above my neck. "I have to wine and dine you first."

"No. No, you don't," I answer blankly. "I volunteer as tribute. Take me. Now. Here. Any way you want."

Ford blows out a breath, clearly trying to contain himself. "Good to know for future reference." He propels himself off the bed, and he has a glimmer in his eye, that victorious smirk never fading. "Babe, get dressed," he orders before he disappears again into his closet. "I'll meet you downstairs."

I prop myself up on my elbows. "What?"

He ducks out of the door mid shirt coming on. "Trust me."

I fall back on the bed, defeated.

He leaves me there, completely frustrated yet curious and amused as to what the hell wine and dine means.

9

FORD

Glancing up from pouring white wine into a glass that rests on the kitchen counter, I notice Brielle walking into the room in only my hoodie and nothing else. I have to do a double take for many reasons—one, how magnificent she looks in my clothes, especially with a sexy look gracing her face. Mostly, I'm watching her stride into my kitchen because I'm amazed that I kept restraint upstairs, and now too, as the sweater hits her knees but leaves enough for the imagination.

But we are a long game, and I need to take my time with her.

Everything is now happening, one domino after another.

"I've poured you a glass." I slide the drink to the edge of the counter where Brielle parks her cute behind on a stool. She's already curling the fabric over her hands because my hoodie drowns her.

Brielle looks at me skeptically. "Right, wining and dining me, because suddenly you have an inkling to go old-fashioned."

I grin to myself before I lean over to capture her mouth for a kiss, one that she willingly gives.

"Quick, hard, and to the point wouldn't have sufficed, baby. And once we get naked later, then we are not leaving my bed," I warn her.

She takes the glass between her fingers, leans back, and hums a sound. "You mention later. I'm not so sure you should assume," she taunts.

I ignore her attempt to tease me and instead look at my watch. "Listen, you should take this wine, go relax by the pool, and I'll be back soon. I need to run next door to Spencer's, and you look a little too flushed to join. Have to give them a bottle of champagne as a congratulations, since they got engaged last night. I had promised Hudson I would stop by, as they are throwing a little celebration before Spencer goes back on the road for a game."

"Is it a full moon? Engagements seem to be happening a lot lately." She sips from her glass.

"You're saying that like you're still engaged. You should take it easy; you need your rest for later."

Brielle looks up from her wine. "That's very considerate."

Leaning over the counter, I take her hands in mine. "We should take a breather before we cross the line that I have every intention of repeating… a lot… tonight."

"I'm trying not to think," she mentions.

That worries me slightly. We wouldn't be the first people to get caught up in lust. "Elle, I won't be a regret."

She is quick to offer me a gentle assuring smile. "I meant, I want to enjoy our time together here, today, tomorrow. I just know there are more factors to consider." Nothing she's saying is soothing. Her finger escapes my hold to tap the back of my hand. "Factors we will consider because we are…"

"More than a one-night fuck."

Her lips purse out, and she tilts her head at an angle. "I guess that's one way of putting it."

I return to standing, bopping her nose with my finger in the process, but I catch her in a daze as she stares at me. "You okay?"

"Yeah. It's just kind of… surreal… this." She points between us. "Kind of takes getting used to but not in a bad way. Kissing you feels natural, very natural, but this dynamic is a little new, or rather it's been so long where we haven't been together-together." She tips her wine glass back.

"Way too long," I lament. "We can go slow," I offer.

"I don't think my body can cope," she casually mentions, with a trace of a smirk on her lips. "Besides, you have to dine me, so dinner is slow enough."

"But that's all physical. What about all the other stuff?"

Our eyes meet briefly for a check-in.

"You mentioned something on the boat that we can have a few days where we make up for lost time, be in our own little world before we face reality, and I think that's our first step."

And maybe she's right.

"Sure," I answer.

Yet, I could jump right in, but I need to let her lead the way. I've already thrown a lot at her. That doesn't mean I'm not going to pull out all the stops to woo her.

That's what I think it is, I respect her so profoundly that I want to give her romance before we get lost in one another.

She isn't any woman, she's the love of my life.

"I'll be back soon," I promise. "Go get comfortable. If you want to study and need something, just look in my office."

She chortles. "There is no way I can concentrate now." Her nails tap on the counter, and she seems to have a moment of clarification. "Are you nervous? Am I throwing you off your game? Is that why I'm not lying in your bed right now?" She's entertained.

I smile awkwardly as I swipe my thumb across my chin. "Uh," I croak out.

"It is, isn't it?" Brielle now softens her voice when she realizes the answer that I've been internally denying.

"Don't be silly. I remember every little detail of your body and have noticed every change since."

Her eyes grow big. "You should probably get out of here because I could take that the wrong way."

"I just meant that I notice when you add highlights in your hair, or you've slept well, when you're in a good mood or bad."

She blushes, and I take it as my cue to walk to her, step between her legs, and cradle her head in my hands.

"I like that it's you who notices."

"Good," I say before I kiss her once more as a parting gift. "I'm not nervous. You just bring out the best of me." One more kiss because I can't resist, and I'm out of there.

———

I HAND Spencer a bottle of champagne as I step into his kitchen where Hudson and Piper are talking with April. The champagne is kind of pointless, as everyone in this room has a closet full of over-the-top and highly priced bottles, but it's the thought that counts.

"I'm not going to stay long, just dropping by, as good neighbors do," I announce.

Spencer slaps a hand on my shoulder. "That's okay, I have to leave in an hour. I have a game this week."

"We know you're busy too, Ford." Piper smiles.

It's then that I notice everyone is staring at me peculiarly, with fixed grins on their faces like they're waiting for something.

"You all okay?" I ask.

"For sure. Anything you care to share?" April wiggles her brows, her blonde hair not moving an inch as she stretches her smile.

I'm trying to read the room but failing miserably.

"We saw a little scene of you carrying someone over your shoulder," Spencer mumbles.

Ah fuck, there is a spot between our property lines that is cleared. We figured we should have a path to each other's yards and docks, for safety since there are kids around.

"Total *The Notebook* vibes," April adds.

Hudson rolls his eyes. "Your plan working?"

"Shouldn't we be discussing April and Spencer?" I suggest.

Spencer and April look at one another then shrug their shoulders. "Nah," they agree in unison.

"Brielle and I are taking some time… for ourselves."

The ladies in the room clap their hands together in excitement, and I'm beginning to wonder if I walked into a bear's den.

"Calm down, ladies." Hudson grins, slightly scared for me.

"Pulling out all the stops, huh?" Spencer asks.

I muss my hair. "Trying. I need to figure out dinner for tonight. Tomorrow, I have a few ideas."

"I'll make your dinner," April is quick to volunteer. She's a nutritionist and cooks daily.

"You just got engaged," I emphasize the obvious.

She is already heading to the fridge. "Yes, and my fiancé has a game to catch. I have a bunch of meals in the freezer. Meat or no meat? Maybe a lasagna?"

"Are you sure?"

April is already pulling out a container from the freezer drawer. "Totally. Here, this is lasagna with pumpkin and sage, the instructions are on the container, and let me go grab some bread dough that I've had resting for days."

"Aren't I a lucky man?" Spencer fondly admires his fiancée, the homemaker.

Spencer's seven-year-old daughter skips into the kitchen, with her pigtails swaying in the air. "Is Connor here?" Excitement is apparent in her voice.

I lean down to her eye level. "Sorry, he's at hockey camp."

"Oh." Her face falls, and she stomps away.

"Someone has a crush. So adorable," Piper notes, with her hands on her chest in admiration.

Spencer and I look at one another, thankful we are not yet near the teenage years.

"We should keep an eye on that, right?" I question.

Spencer gives me a cartoonish look. "Don't remind me."

April arrives with a cloth bag full of food. Handing it to me, I'm quick to notice she went overboard, including a bag of salad.

"This is way too kind." I take the tote.

"Nah, it's fine. Besides, I expect a full report later in the week or maybe I will have my dog *accidentally* stroll into your yard, and oops, I need to go rescue him. Would seven be an ideal time for that?" she jokes.

I have to smile at her humor, and I'm thankful that I have such great neighbors. We look out for one another.

"Thank you. I don't mean to dash already, but I really just wanted to say congrats in person real quick." I open my arms to hug April, then Spencer gets a side hug.

A quick round of goodbyes, but, of course, Hudson has to

be the last to give me the older-and-wiser advice that he loves to dish out.

"Opportunity is what we make of it. Grab it when you can and don't let go." His advice isn't new, but I appreciate him reminding us when he can.

"I have no intention of letting it go," I promise.

RETURNING TO MY HOUSE, I put everything away for later then throw on my swim trunks before I head out back to find Brielle lying on a lounger beside the pool in a black bikini and sunhat as she reads a massive book with a highlighter in hand. She is giving studying a whirl, I guess.

I've seen her in a bikini a few times over the years, but now I'm allowed to look and fantasize without guilt, and I love that.

"Ditched the air conditioner and my hoodie?" I say as I whip off my t-shirt.

She glances up from the book and smiles. "Really? Yet again, you feel a shirt isn't necessary?" I have to grin because she's calling me out. "Illinois summer is good to us this year, so I'm going to enjoy this eighty-five-degree no-wind weather. We know winter is coming at some point. I thought I would try to study, but I haven't made a dent."

I sit on the lounger next to her. "Good, you should relax. My sister sent me some photos of Connor today at camp." I pull out my phone and swipe the screen to show Brielle, who instantly smiles wide.

"He's a cutie." Connor is wearing skates and is holding his hockey stick as he waits for his turn to hit between the orange cones. "Growing so fast."

"Yeah, he is."

We look at one another with affection, as there is never a moment that we don't look elated when discussing our boy.

I decide to put my phone to the side so we can focus on each other. We can be selfish and not focus on gushing the praises of our son for one afternoon. Today is about us.

"So, how about at six we have dinner?" I suggest.

Brielle closes her book. "What's on the menu?"

"It's a surprise."

"You're cooking?"

"Kind of." Half the truth. I'm turning the oven on at least.

She nibbles her bottom lip, trying not to smile, but I can tell that she's happy. "Okay."

"Shall I go grab more wine?"

"No, I'll save my intake for later, plus it's a little too warm out for wine."

"You're warm?" I stand up and offer my hand. "Come on, let's go for a swim."

Brielle's fingers carefully walk into my palm, but I grab hold of her wrist and yank her up, causing her hat to fall. Quickly, I hook my arm under her knees to carry her.

"Don't you dare throw me in," she giggles.

"Wouldn't dream of it." I grin.

She clings to my neck. "Liar."

And she's right, I drop her in the deep end and dive in after.

We both submerge under the water before swimming to each other. With water swooshing around us, I love the way Brielle brings her arms around my neck before wrapping her legs around me. She knows I'm her anchor both in the pool and life.

Our bodies are close, and it feels so damn right, yet tantalizing. This will be a struggle not to play with the tie behind her neck, but it will make tonight even better.

"Hi," she says shyly.

"Hey." I dip my head down to kiss her neck. "Look at us."

"Crazy."

"Nah, crazy is waiting this long."

She gives me knowing eyes. "Maybe."

I can't read what is hinted in that word, but I don't get too worried as she kisses me with intention.

For the next hour, we just wade in the pool, splashing around and chatting about the Bar exam, Lake Spark, and the training facility that I'm running. It's easy and relaxing. In a way, no different from the way we've been the last ten years, except for the fact I get to touch her, hold her, and kiss her. It's a change but welcome.

We were in a good mood when we both went our separate ways to shower and change. I threw on a fresh t-shirt and jeans before I worked my magic in the kitchen and outside. I've dated, sure, but I've never romanced someone the way I am for Brielle.

By the time I have everything set up, Brielle arrives down the stairs barefoot but in a black cotton dress that clings to her and stops mid-thigh.

Her mouth parts open with a gasp when she walks outside to the edge of the patio where I'm lighting a few candles on the table to keep the mosquitos away. This is the perfect spot to overlook the lake and sunset. My Bluetooth plays music; I'm really on a Hovvdy kick lately, and it fits us for this moment.

"You did this?" She walks to the table. "It's beautiful, romantic, and a little surprising. But unexpected is easy to do, as no part of today is how I was planning my week to go." She notices the warm lasagna, salad, and bread. "You cooked?"

"I might have had April's help so I won't poison you." I bring her chair out to help her in.

"I'm slightly relieved with that news," she admits and slides onto the chair. "Thank you."

We have white wine in a bucket. Olive Owl, her favorite, and I get an abundance of wine supply since Hudson's son married into the family that owns the brand. I'm quick to pick up the bottle and get busy with the cork.

"A toast," I suggest.

"Depends on what we're toasting," she playfully challenges as she picks up the wine glasses on the table and holds them out for me.

I think for a second. This isn't a new beginning because I don't want us to erase what was, especially since it includes our son. I pop the cork and begin to pour. "To timing." It's the best I can do.

"Maybe. Or to waiting. Maybe we'll figure out if we're worth it," she counters with hope in her tone.

Optimism is something we share, which is why we clink our glasses to celebrate the night ahead.

FORD

Brielle sets her fork down and looks up at me as she finishes her bite. "This was delicious. I wish I had the ability to cook like this."

I throw my napkin to the side. "You're fine. Connor loves your mashed potatoes."

She laughs to herself. "Not exactly earth-shattering to make."

"I don't know. You have to get the ratio of butter and milk right or it doesn't have the right consistency. Or at least that is what Connor tells me when I attempt to make them."

There it is. Sentimental fondness gracing her face.

"I love him so much," she reflects as she takes her wine glass in her hand. Leaning back in the chair, she looks out over the lake which is nearly dark since the sun disappeared over the pines on the horizon. "You won't let him skate on the lake when it freezes, right?"

"Of course not. I'll take him to a pond nearby or the training facility. Where's that coming from?"

"Nothing. It's just a beautiful lake, and for some reason, I thought about winter and how the lake freezes sometimes, plus you play hockey, Connor loves hockey. My mind spins a little."

"Ah yes, mom instinct."

She throws me a playful glare. "It's a superpower."

"I have a few superpowers too."

Brielle folds her arms onto the table. "Oh yeah? Do tell."

"Restraint, endurance, and pleasure," I confidently inform her before throwing back a sip of wine.

I notice she blows out a small breath between her lips and tucks a strand of hair behind her ear, but her smile never wavers. "I'm sure."

Our eyes hold, with the light of the candles offering a dim reflection. "There is too much distance between us," I inform her.

"You mean the table?" She points down to double-check.

"Yeah."

Her fingers trace the top of her wine glass. "I might consider finding a new seat if you tell me the truth about something."

My ears perk up, as I'm not entirely sure what's on her mind. "What would that be?"

"Why did it have to be Lake Spark where you set your roots down?"

I shrug my shoulder. "It's a great little town, a perfect spot to build a house, great for winter and summer… and it reminds me of you."

Her eyes flick up. "You decided to build a house here already a few years ago."

"Exactly," I confess. "Remembering our time together kept me going. Just like a compass, you always go back to the starting point." Her cheeks tighten, and she seems to have gone mute from my revelation. "I think deep down you figured it out too, otherwise you wouldn't have asked me just now."

The lids of her eyes close for a few beats as she collects her thoughts. When her eyes open, I see it all. I know she is affected, because water swells in the bottom of her eyes, but mostly I recognize the agreement hinted in her look.

"Now tell me the truth." It's my turn.

"What?"

"If I didn't make this week happen, would you have ever told me the truth about how you feel?"

Brielle stands up and takes a few steps to look out over the lake. "Truthfully? I don't know. I got little pieces of you, and sometimes I thought that would be enough to keep me from falling apart."

"Little pieces?" I ask as I grab the bottle to pour us more wine.

"You know, seeing you at pick-ups and a few moments that we just... I don't know." She glances back at me. "Like a few months ago when Connor had the flu, and we agreed it wasn't a good idea for him to go to your house, so you came over to see him and then..."

"I slept on the couch until his fever went down," I finish her sentence.

She nods. "I knew you visited for Connor, but you were in my house, sleeping, just there... so close." She covers her face with her hand, as if she could hide. "Fuck, I just admitted that."

I have to smile to myself. "Sorry I didn't take my shirt off," I say in an attempt to make her laugh, but then my face grows stoic because I know what she's saying. "I pretended to sleep."

"What?"

"I pretended to sleep," I repeat. "I couldn't sleep a wink

knowing you were in the other room in your bed. I think I stayed more because I knew it would be the next best thing. I got to be near you for a night."

She laughs, swiping away a tear. "Are we horrible parents? We had a hidden agenda while our son had a fever."

"We're allowed to put ourselves first sometimes. Besides, his fever was going down, and we had the situation under control."

Brielle slowly walks to my side of the table. "I think I'm going to move seats now." Her smile is sultry.

"Oh yeah?" I lean back, ready to welcome her.

She sits on my lap and loops her arms around my neck. "Right here, if you don't mind."

I tip my chin up to get a better angle to kiss her lips. "I insist."

Cementing our lips together, it's Brielle this time who kisses with determination, her fingers raking into the hair on the back of my neck. She has me captivated and at her mercy. Yet, I have the courage to sneak my tongue into her mouth to show her that I'll lead us if she lets me.

Our tongues duel before her lips create a trail of hurried kisses down my jaw and neck.

This is it.

We snap.

There is no going back.

"We can skip the brownies, right?" I husk as my hands roam her body.

She pulls away for a second with a serious look. "Wait, there are chocolate brownies?"

"Uhm… yes." I'm concerned that her love for dessert is one step higher on her pedestal for me.

Her look tells me that I'm being brushed to the side, but then her face breaks. "I guess they can wait."

Relief hits me, and I'm quick to usher her up, never letting go of our interlaced fingers. "Let me blow out the candles." I lean over to extinguish the flames.

"Fire safety, so responsible," she chides.

"I'm a dad," I proudly counter.

Brielle yanks my arm to lead us inside.

———

OUR HANDS DON'T DROP as we slowly walk into my bedroom, and I'm not quite sure who is leading whom. The problem with slow is that it ups the ante and makes the realization of what we are doing more profound. The air is thick with anticipation, and the beating of my heart feels strong.

When we are near my bed, I reel Brielle into me and wrap my arm around her waist. "You okay?" I have to smile.

"Perfect."

"Not nervous?"

Her lips quirk out. "I mean, it's not every day that Ford Spears, star hockey player, takes me to bed, but ya know, there are worse hardships in life."

A laugh escapes me before I remind her of the obvious. "You're the only one that I've ever wanted."

"Okay, now you're setting the bar high. I might be a little nervous now." She wryly smiles and then jabs my chest with her finger. "It's been a while since we did this. Together. I mean, you and me."

"We were teenagers."

"I got pregnant."

"Oh, we're already there? It was three sons, right? I guess if I aim right…" I tease her. I'm following her cues because she seems to be anxious.

She swats me playfully. "We don't need to worry, I have an IUD. Without going into detail, my priorities haven't been on dating lately. So, if we're good on all fronts, then we are set."

With my fingers, I comb her hair away from her face. "We're good. Look at us being responsible adults."

"I'm stalling."

"I noticed."

Her beautiful eyes lock with mine. "Is it crazy that my body feels like it might explode? Because this has only ever been a dream, and now it's a reality."

"This afternoon you didn't want me to stop."

"I know, but every minute more with you and I realize how deep we are."

I tighten my hold with our fingers, bringing her hand up to my lips for a feathery kiss. "Does that scare you?"

"The opposite."

I gently kiss her lips to ground us, but my attempt to do soft is thwarted by Brielle returning my kiss with what I can only describe as passion. It's fervent, electrifying, and when she invites me to follow her as she walks backward, it's a confirmation that I don't need to go slow.

"I want you," she rasps right before she drops to sit on the mattress.

"There hasn't been a day I stopped wanting you." I begin to pull my shirt up at the same time my knee lands on the bed. With my shirt thrown to the floor, I guide Brielle back until she's under me.

Kissing her, my hand skims the fabric of her dress until I find the hem. Dragging the fabric up, her knee moves which means I'm better aligned with her center.

"You drive me crazy." My voice is gruff.

Her body arches up which causes her dress to bunch

around her waist, and her panty-covered pussy presses against my hard length. "I bet I can make you go insane."

I pin her wrists to the mattress, which makes Brielle giggle and squirm, especially as I nibble the base of her neck, trailing my lips along her collarbone. "Keep your hands where they are," I warn her.

Making sure she watches me, I begin to unbutton her dress, and the moment all the buttons are free, I hiss a sound of pure admiration that she is lying in my bed with a matching black lace bra and panties. "Gorgeous," I whisper.

"Take more off." Her hands reach for the buckle of my jeans.

Quickly, I push her hands away. "Arms on the bed."

"Ooh, bossy."

I flash her a fake unimpressed look before I step out of my jeans and return to her. I slide down her bra strap and trace her skin until I reach her breast. My tongue darts out to twirl around her lace-covered nipple, and her body curves from enjoyment.

I peer up to see her watching me. I repeat the movement on her other breast before I move both cups down to twist her nipples between my fingers to play with her.

She moans and breathes heavily, which only encourages me to kiss between the valley of her breasts and lower. Giving a few extra popcorn kisses around her belly button and then moving below her navel.

Brielle writhes under me, and her sweet scent of desire hits my nose as I travel over her mound. I nuzzle over her soaked lace. It's intoxicating, and I want more, which is why I lap my tongue up her panties, getting a taste.

Brielle claws the sheets in surprise and moans a breath.

"I need more," I growl. Peeling her panties off, I dive right back to where I was. Spreading her lips, I lick, taking a moment to swirl and explore. I could do this for hours; I only need to feast on her for survival.

"Ford," she cries.

I dip my tongue inside her center, before swiping back up to her clit, but I pause. "You're ready. Are you aching for me?"

"Yes," she responds and brings her hands to my head. "Don't stop."

"We're just getting started," I promise. My tongue flicks her clit, and my finger arrives at her center to explore her wet channel.

I suck and lick her, until she is panting and near her edge.

"I'm almost there."

I work harder, find a rhythm, and keep her begging for more.

Then she's convulsing against my mouth, and I slow down. I take a moment to enjoy her taste of subtle sweetness and inhale her. I keep my tongue flat against her clit until I feel she's steady.

Brielle is trying to capture her breath, but I decide to kiss her anyways. She seems taken aback when she whimpers a sound, but then realizes her taste is on my lips, and she gets greedy.

My hand travels between her legs to feel her open and wet. She joins me in exploration, giving herself a stroke, but only once because she moves my boxer briefs and takes hold of my cock.

"Inside of me, please," she pleads, ensuring our eyes stay connected.

"Get comfortable, baby."

I invite her to scoot back onto my bed until her head rests on my pillow, and she unclasps her bra while I discard my boxer briefs.

Gliding my fingers up her inner thigh, I find my destination. Settling between her legs, the tip of my cock slides between her, taunting her clit and driving me feral.

"I'll start slow," I promise.

I begin to fill her, and she gasps, but our eyes catch and a reassuring smile spreads on her lips.

"You're mine again," I breathe into her neck.

"I was always yours."

Inch by inch, I enter her, waiting for her cues, which are difficult to read, as her eyes remain committed and filled with what I believe is love.

I interweave our hands against the pillow by her ear, dragging myself in and out just enough to drive us wild.

"It's okay, you can go deeper," she encourages.

I stay inside of her but stop moving, and instead, I take the moment to bring my hand to her face to brush my thumb against her lips. Brielle is the one I'll spend my life with, I know it, which is why I deliver her request. We get lost in this moment until we are riding a wave that involves two sweaty bodies, moving together, locked in a gaze, because the future is ours for the taking.

BRIELLE

I wake feeling fulfilled.

Stretching out my arms and stirring in Ford's bed, I make no mistake that I am in his arms, and he has been holding me all night after we went a few rounds.

He smiles down at me. "Hey, beautiful." His voice is hoarse.

"How long have you been awake?" I yawn.

"A little while. I'm still getting used to sleeping in after years of waking early for training."

His hands rub warmth into my arm near my elbow. I inhale his scent of morning musk, and I enjoy it because it means I'm in *his* bed.

I should pinch myself to confirm that this is reality, but I feel his cock wide awake against the back of my thigh, and I know that this isn't a dream.

"After last night, don't you need a little extra sleep?" I wonder.

He smirks at me before he adjusts our bodies so that I can rest my head against his chest. I eagerly draw circles on his pec with my fingers because his toned physique is a master-piece that I like to touch.

"I'd rather watch you naked in my bed."

"So be it, but I'm not going easy on you this morning," I warn him.

Ford's fingers caress my back as we lie together, perfectly intent.

"I thought we could head into town for some breakfast, then I need to head to Connor's camp."

My head perks up. "You're seeing Connor today?"

Ford squeezes me closer. "You too. You're coming with me if you don't mind watching me teach a group of ten-year-olds."

I smile. "I'd love to."

"Good. Then we'll head to Jolly Joe's and make our way to the training center after."

"Ooh, you sound like you have us on a tight schedule," I note.

Ford snorts a laugh. "No, but we should be out of the house in about an hour."

A mischievous grin overtakes my face, I can feel my lips curl. I walk my fingers up Ford's chest. "If we have an hour, then I think there is something we can work on."

Ford flips me to my back with a satisfied smirk of his own. "What could that be?"

"We have a lot of time to make up for, so I think…" I wiggle and feel between us to grip his cock, and his head falls low as he enjoys my hand wrapped around him to give him a stroke.

"I couldn't agree more." He slithers his body out of my hold and down the mattress, disappearing under the duvet. I grab hold of the duvet to inspect what he's doing, only to find him parting my thighs open and staring at my pussy. "Just checking how swollen you are and ensuring my mark stayed inside of you."

Fire ignites inside of me from his words. My nipples harden, and my body is awakened with extra sensitivity, including the air that hits my nipples.

"And," I breathe. "Do you approve?" My voice is uneven, as I'm so heightened and I need his touch.

Ford swipes my clit with the pad of his thumb. "I want to fill you up again."

"I want that too." I lick my lips.

I can't take it anymore, and I scoot up to sitting and encourage Ford to swap places. I straddle him with my knee on each side of his hips. Taking his cock in my palm, I wrap my fingers around him to give him a few pumps before aligning him with my opening and sliding on top of him. We both moan at the same time.

"Take what you want from me," Ford encourages and squares my hips with his hands.

"Everything feels too good." My lids go heavy, and my back arches, with my hair falling behind me and my breasts on offer.

Ford sits up, brushing his lips along the curve of my breast. "That's because only my cock should be inside of you. I was made for you, and you were made for me. Now be a good girl and tell me that you understand that only I will ever make you come."

I think I might faint. When Ford says these things, he has a determined edge in his tone, a sort of territorial order that he likes to remind me of, and it only turns me on more, especially when I feel him slide in and out of me.

"I understand."

"Say it, Elle."

"Only you will ever make me come," I promise.

He growls before he sucks on a nipple, while his fingers dig into the flesh of my hips.

I continue to move, bouncing on top of him, and Ford meets me on every thrust. I fall back onto my arms, but I can still see him inside of me. Ford brings his finger to my clit as he takes over setting our speed, and I clench around him, with the world blurring around us.

"Let go, and I will fill you up. I want you to feel me inside of you the whole day," he tells me.

I nod as I circle my hips around him, following his demand. "Ford," I call out as I tremble, and he is quick to catch me.

My orgasm comes easy, and that's mostly because this man knows my body. He feels my needs because everything I want leads me back to him.

———

FORD BRINGS a cup of coffee to his lips where he's sitting next to me in our booth at Jolly Joe's. The soda shop-styled cafe always has something for everyone, from milkshakes to a cinnamon roll with coffee. It's quiet this morning, so the subtle sound of doo-wop can be heard while we look out the big windows onto Main Street.

"I don't remember you drinking coffee. Something about caffeine killing your hockey mojo," I remark as I play with the spoon in my coffee mug.

He wraps his arm around my shoulders. "I no longer have to worry about hockey demands. I run my own show. Besides, you know why I really ordered a coffee here."

I smile brightly as I dip my spoon into my coffee and scoop up a red jellybean. "Because of the ridiculous idea that someone had to add jellybeans to coffee?" It's a Jolly Joe's specialty.

"You never know what color you'll get."

Looking down at the food in front of us, I question how we will get through all of this. We have almost every item on the menu; pancakes, eggs, bacon, cinnamon rolls. This entire week has turned into a week of sex and food, which in retrospect is not a bad thing.

"Remember when you used to take me here for ice cream?" I dig into my cinnamon roll with the side of my fork.

Ford sets his coffee down. "Turtle sundae with butterscotch, not caramel, and an extra cherry on top."

"And you were chocolate with marshmallow."

"We didn't spend much time amongst civilization, though."

I give Ford side-eye and raise my brows.

He rumbles a sound under his breath. "I want to take you to our place. We can go tomorrow."

"You mean the lagoon? I'm sure there's a new set of teenagers who made a claim that it's their spot."

Ford chomps on a bacon slice. "I'll pay them to scram and remind them to keep it safe."

I laugh at how ridiculous that sounds, but I know that it's something Ford would do.

"A few days ago, I would have been petrified to go there. It's too overwhelming with memories of you. But now… it sounds perfectly fitting," I announce and take another giant bite from my cinnamon roll.

"Good. So today we will see Connor, take it easy, and you can study if you want, and then tomorrow, we'll make it a day."

"Sounds good." I move my plate to the side and feel I

need to address the obvious. "Seeing Connor today, you know that he—"

Ford quickly interjects. "Can't know that we're kind of a thing again?"

"Yeah, exactly that. We shouldn't confuse him."

He looks at me, slightly irritated, his gaze piercing. "I get it. But make no mistake, we are playing the long game."

I roll my eyes. "Okay, but it requires a little more thought than that. You said give this a week. I mean, I don't even live in Lake Spark."

"Yes, but next summer Connor is switching schools anyway for middle school, so you both can come to Lake Spark."

"And what about my career? I mean, I'm not exactly sure there are a lot of job prospects here for me as hopefully a new lawyer," I highlight the apparent, and I feel like I'm tainting our last amazing 24 hours.

Ford angles his body to me and takes my hand. "First off, no hope, you *will* be a new lawyer soon." I appreciate that he has always been my biggest cheerleader. "And job prospects, I don't know. I'm sure my training facility needs more people on our legal staff."

I shake my head. "No, I'm not going down that route."

"This time we won't let anything or anyone get in our way," he promises, and I love the faith in his voice.

I attempt to smile, but deep down I have a fear that something will get in our way.

"Come on, eat a little more. You need your strength." There is pure sexiness in his voice.

We finish up our breakfast and take a little walk on Main Street, as we have time to spare. I see Piper in her boutique, and she waves at me through the window.

"I should go in and say hi."

Ford steps back and holds his hands up. "Go for it. I'll stay out here."

I look at him peculiarly. "Why?"

"She's my neighbor and Hudson's wife, so I need to remain somewhat respectable. I can't go inside her boutique with you and not go crazy."

"It's just a bouti… ahh." My brain catches up, and I roll my lips in as I try not to grin. "A lingerie boutique."

Ford slides his hand into my hair to pull me in for a kiss. "But go in there and have fun. Use the credit card for it."

I burst out with a laugh. "You want me to use the credit card you gave me, which is for Connor and things he needs, to buy lingerie?"

"Why not? I like providing for my family." He can't control his grin.

I wave him off. "I'll be quick."

I don't look back and head straight into Piper's boutique. The bell chimes over my head and the door closes behind me.

Piper is behind the counter, opening a box, with her daughter asleep in her stroller in the corner.

"How is life with our favorite hockey player? You both look cute walking hand in hand down Main. By the way, there is a rumor that Margo wanted to buy out the florist for your upcoming wedding." Piper has a knowing grin as she focuses on her task.

I assess the array of lingerie and pajamas in the store. I'm not sure where to focus, everything is either beautiful, sexy, or cozy.

"Remind me to fix that scenario. And Ford and me? It's… well," I say as I touch the fabric of a red nightie.

"That's a good choice, but if I may be a little bold, then I would suggest the deep purple color."

My hand retreats back like I touched a hot pan. "Oh, I just

came in to say hi and check to see how Grace's skin is going."

Piper walks to her daughter and smiles. "She's doing better, thank you. Sleeping like a little angel. Her bath with the oat oil really helped." Piper steps in my direction. "Let me repay you with something."

"Don't be silly. Advice is free," I protest.

Piper holds a finger in the air. "Exactly, advice is free." She walks to the corner and reaches behind a rack of clothes on hangers to pull out an item hanging in the back. When she holds it up, my eyes nearly bug out. It's a bra-and-panty set with stocking suspenders, black with bright pink edging.

"I can't wear that!"

"Of course you can."

I shake my head in astonishment.

"It's always fun to shake things up."

My mouth opens but no words come out. "I guess… well, Ford and I, we're…"

Piper patiently waits for my explanation.

"We were teenagers when we were first together, kind of sweet. Now, we're adults with a kid." I laugh.

"Exactly. Show him you're a woman now. That's my advice. Remind him that everything is different, and that can make things even better." She holds the set out in front of her. "I think I got your sizing right."

Blowing out a breath, I'm not sure what to say. "Why not." I throw my hands up into the air. "But let me at least pay."

"Nonsense." Piper is already pulling out tissue paper and a bag.

"Thank you," I give up and make a mental note to give back to her in some way at a later moment.

"You're very welcome. Happy neighbor, happy life, right?"

"I'm not your neighbor," I remind her with a smile.

"But Ford is, and he has been pining for you for forever." She hands me the bag.

Taking the bag, I can only agree. "Me too, if I'm being honest."

Saying our goodbyes, I make it back to Main Street to find Ford leaning against a tree with his shades on. That is until he sees I have a bag in my hand, then he propels off the tree and tips his sunglasses down to the tip of his nose.

"I'm curious," he firmly states.

"Me too." I laugh nervously.

He pulls me close and tries to steal the bag hanging off my fingertips, but I don't let him succeed.

"Naughty us will have to wait. We need to go see someone important," I remind him with a fake stern look.

Ford growls into my neck before stepping to the side, taking my hand, and walking us in the direction of the car.

"Our son," he confirms.

FORD

L etting go of Brielle's hand when we entered the rink was a difficult task, but I get it.

Mixed signals for Connor are something neither of us intend to do.

Walking down the main hall, there are ice rinks on each side. This place also has other sports. Hudson even trains his football team in a field nearby in the summer.

"This place is impressive," Brielle compliments.

I scratch my thumb over my chin which has some stubble since I didn't want to waste any time this morning. Elle is taking a chance on us, admitting truths, and letting me back into her life the way I want to be in hers. So yeah, there was no time for shaving.

"Thanks. After the summer when Connor is back at school, I'll get my head busy with logistics and planning. We have a lot of staff to handle here, so there will be a lot of meetings, I'm sure."

"But here you are now, volunteering to teach a class for the kids." She smiles with the praise.

"I would like to think even if I didn't have a son that I

would still have found myself here. And if I don't like it, then maybe I'll coach college hockey. There is something about eager athletes that would keep me on my toes."

"I could see that. The nearest college to Lake Spark is ironically Hollows."

"I may have noticed." We walk side by side, our shoulders occasionally grazing. "Connor will be on a break soon, and then you can see him."

"I guess I need to get used to this. I don't see Connor giving up hockey any time soon."

"You resent hockey?"

She bobs her head side to side. "I could say it took you away from me, but hockey is part of your identity and what you enjoy. I knew as soon as I discovered we were having a boy that he would probably want to follow in your footsteps. Don't get me wrong, I would be thrilled if he said hockey wasn't for him and he would rather try theater or violin. I get scared that as he gets older, the game gets more… intense."

I touch her shoulder to comfort her. "I understand, but right now, he is still a junior and wears lots of padding, and they take it easy. It's no different to any other sport."

"Except he is wearing skates on ice, and hockey moms scare me. I need to go full-on grizzly mama bear around hockey moms," she tells me in a neutral tone.

I laugh at her statement. "You're the hottest hockey mom there is."

Brielle shoots me a warning glare. "No flirting here."

Up ahead I see someone I know and nod my head. "Hey, Declan," I call out.

Declan is my former teammate; he was new to the team this year, and I took him under my wing. He is also worth billions, thanks to his family and investments. He has proven everyone wrong by demonstrating he earned a spot on the team by pure talent, and lucky for them, he still has a few years left to play.

"Hey, Ford." He walks to me and shakes my hand. His eyes are immediately drawn to Brielle at my side.

Clearing my throat, I set my hand on Brielle's lower back. As much as I would consider Declan a friend, I have no problem giving him the stay-the-fuck-away-from-my-woman stare, because his bachelor status doesn't exactly thrill me, especially since I'm about to hit the ice and leave Brielle alone in the stands.

"You just gave an hour to the kids?"

"Yeah." Declan's blue eyes float between us in slight confusion.

I explain, "Brielle is here to check on *our* son."

Brielle smiles tightly.

"It's good to see you again. Connor is a natural talent," Declan compliments.

"I'll never get tired of hearing that," Brielle responds.

"Those kids wore me out. Good luck," he voices.

I fold my arms over my chest, amused. "It's worth it. Thanks again for volunteering."

"Gets me bragging rights on my next date." He is completely joking because, underneath his steely exterior, I'm sure there is a heart of gold.

I look at my watch and internally groan. "Listen, I would love to hear who the woman of the month is, but I need to grab my skates from my office. Don't make me regret this but can you walk Brielle to the rink? My sister Violet will meet her there."

Declan is already offering Brielle his arm. "My plea-sure. Happy to volunteer to take care of your precious goods."

"Oh." Brielle seems taken aback by his arm offer. "Thank

you." She's unsure yet entertained, and they both look at me, knowing this scene drives me coconuts.

But alas, it doesn't take much for my inner caveman to come out when it involves Elle, and everyone knows it.

———

HOCKEY WAS MY LIFE. From the moment I tried on my first pair of skates. There is something about gliding along the ice or the sound of the blade that just brings me peace. Hockey itself is a game where every second is different. It's fast-paced and energizing, yet every move feels like a risk because you don't know how the puck will slide.

But this group of ten-year-olds are slightly different. They're learning more about handling a hockey stick, making goals, and the number of orange cones on the ice are enough to make someone go blind. Point is, they're still kids. Brielle is right, though, soon the game will change as Connor gets older.

The group are all sitting on a side bench snacking on oranges and granola bars. It doesn't take long for me to spot Connor at the end hugging his mom. I skate on over to hear their conversation.

"I'm so happy you're enjoying your week here. I've missed you like crazy." Brielle touches Connor's face.

Our son is the perfect mix of Brielle and me. Connor has Brielle's hair and eyes, although Brielle swears Connor has my eyes, but his mouth is for sure mine. His current haircut is a little too short for my liking, but he is only ten. Brielle always says he is as handsome as can be. I like to think that my boy will be breaking and mending hearts for years to come.

He shakes her hand away. "You came all the way to Lake

Spark to see me?" Connor asks his mom.

Brielle pauses for a second, quickly catching me in her view. "Something like that. I'm getting ready for our little family week together after camp."

"Did you see my new room?" He seems excited.

"I did. Perfect for my little prince."

Connor groans. "Don't say that."

Brielle plants her hand on her hip. "Getting too big to be my little prince, huh?"

"I was already too big like two years ago."

I laugh and rustle his hair. "Newsflash, kiddo, there is no age limit for your mom to call you whatever she wants."

"Great." He sounds unenthused.

"Where's your Aunt Violet?" I haven't seen her yet.

"Had to run to the office. She said she'll take me to see a PG-13 movie tonight."

Brielle gives me a pointed look.

I tightly smile. "I'm sure she meant *after* checking in with us."

"Are you going to do drills today?"

"Yeah, I am. Remember I'm coach out there on the ice, not Dad."

Connor bites into his granola bar and speaks with a full mouth. "I know. I mean, every kid here knows already, but fine, we can play along."

Brielle laughs and checks Connor's water bottle, her habit from ensuring he has every snack and packed lunch at the ready. "I'll just be watching in the stands."

"Nobody else's family is watching."

"That's because nobody else here has a dad who runs this place."

"Gah, fine. Just don't embarrass me."

I place my hand on Connor's shoulder. "You're truly a

delight today. Remember to be kind to everyone, say thank you, be grateful, and never forget that your dad has the ability to take your game system away," I remind him.

Connor's face falls. "I know."

"I promise I'll stay quiet. You won't even know I'm here," Brielle proclaims as she squeezes Connor's arm.

"Thanks. I should go back to the group."

"Of course," Brielle nods.

The moment Connor has his back turned, I skate closer to the wall so only Brielle can hear. "Breathe. He's just being a kid." Brielle does her best to keep her eyes wide open because I can tell she is about to break.

"He's no longer a little boy. When did that happen? I feel like pre-teen hell is hitting us early," she mumbles.

"Trust me, he will still have his moments where he needs you. It'll also be better when he isn't around other kids," I promise.

I see my sister walking down the steps of the rink. She smiles, and I wave back. Nobody ever figures out we're related. She's petite with black hair and looks nothing like me.

"Hey, Violet," I call out.

Brielle looks over her shoulder and turns to offer Violet a hug. "Hey."

"Sorry, I had to run to the office to check that the next snack will arrive at three instead of two." Violet looks between us. "Got to see Connor?"

"Yeah, he hates that I'm here." Brielle pouts for dramatics.

Violet touches her arm. "If it's any consolation, I'm only cool if I supply pizza. I can't even sway him with watching the Mighty Ducks movies anymore. That was a total win for me. Hockey for Connor and Joshua Jackson."

Brielle touches Violet's shoulder in agreement. "Oh yeah, totally forgot he's in that. So, right, Connor is too old for everything now."

Ignoring their nostalgia, I tell my sister, "Thanks again for helping out."

My sister shrugs. "Kind of needed something to do while I figure out my life. Speaking of which, Margo phoned me to ask what kind of flowers you both might like for your wedding?" She gives Brielle and me a confused look.

Brielle croaks out a sound and pretends to cough.

I rub the back of my neck. "What did you say?"

"That I'll get back to her." Violet is waiting for further explanation. "Something you two need to share?"

"Do you think she told Mom and Dad?" I ask awkwardly. As much as we are adults, we all know my dad will have an opinion on any reunion between Brielle and me.

Violet looks at Brielle for a clue then back to me. "No. She barely talks to them, and why aren't you telling me that Margo lost the plot?"

"Yeah, Ford, why aren't you?" Brielle gives me a cheeky smirk.

Looking at my watch, I pretend it's time. "Wow, look at that. Need to start warming up."

Violet looks back and forth between us, tilting her head to study Elle's vacant finger. "Okay, no engagement ring. Why are you two acting so… oh my God, you two are totally hooking up again," she loudly whispers, her face completely entertained.

I hold my hand up to indicate for her to quiet down. "You're my sister. We are not having this conversation."

"This is why I'm babysitting my favorite little devil, isn't it? You were really serious about your get-Brielle-to-Lake-Spark plan."

Brielle swipes a hand through her hair. "Wow, was I really the last one to figure out his agenda?"

My sister gives Brielle raised brows. "Oh please, Connor or no Connor, you really think you both would have lasted more than a day during 'family time at the lake house?'" Violet uses air quotes.

Brielle attempts to say something but fails.

"Don't you have emails to check? Maybe fill a water cooler? What am I paying you for again?"

"Big brother can't handle the hard facts? Fine." Violet takes two steps then pauses and whirls her finger in the air. "I'm not leaving because you told me to. I'm leaving because I have emails to answer and need to show Declan where he can connect his laptop."

"Oh yeah, Declan had to answer his phone. He said he'll call you later," Brielle informs me.

I shake my head. "Violet, just take Declan to an office. Don't try anything, Declan knows you are to be treated like a sister."

"Lucky me. I will show him to your office, but I'm doing it because I have job responsibilities, not because my brother is giving me orders." She tosses her hair behind her shoulders and stomps up the steps.

Brielle bursts out laughing. "The maturity between you two is really next-level."

"It's the fun of having a sibling." Looking down at my skates, I glide back and forth in place, but when I glance up, I notice a funny look on Brielle's face. "You okay?"

"Totally."

"Liar."

She looks around, checking that nobody notices us. "I like your look. Jeans and skates with a sweater on, it's my favorite."

Assessing myself, I'd say that she has good taste. My jaw flexes side to side. "Truth?"

She nods in agreement.

"Have you always been checking me out every time I hit the ice?"

"Maybe," she plays coy, but it's obvious.

I lick my lips and grin to myself. "Thought so." I lean over the wall. "And you are the hot hockey mom I'm always checking out."

"Thought so," she repeats my words.

Skating back, I don't tear my sight away from her until I have to turn to skate forward.

It never gets old, Elle watching me on the ice. In truth, she gave me the drive to play harder and better. Now? She makes me excited for my next chapter on and off the ice.

The kids all pile onto the ice again and skate a few laps. A few times I catch Connor watching his mom sitting in the stands. When the kids come to circle around me, I'm setting down one more cone. We're going to practice passing the puck side to side.

I notice my son staring at me more intently than normal. I give him a wink, but he rolls back his shoulder.

Fuck me, I wish I could freeze time so he can't grow anymore.

Sometimes I wonder when he's older if he will ever puzzle the pieces of Brielle's and my life together, connecting the dots that we sacrificed a lot for him, but he'll appreciate that we love him so much which is why we lost time. Most of all, I wonder if he will look back to now when his parents decided that the puzzle can only be completed if we're together.

Because that's what we're doing.

13

BRIELLE

olding my sun hat, I breathe in the fresh air and take in the sunlight hitting my face and skin, as I'm only in my bikini with a mesh cover-up. Ford is driving the boat across the lake. Luckily, this time we are on the speedboat and not the rowboat, which I am fairly convinced he used the other day because he knew I wouldn't be able to row us back if I tried to escape.

Staring at Ford, my mouth forms a half-smile. He looks good with his sunglasses on, no shirt, and steering the boat. He's the man I've always wanted, and he is now within my reach.

"Daydreaming?" he asks as he turns the wheel.

"I'm that obvious, huh?"

"Yeah. I hope you're thinking about when I get to see whatever is in that bag from Piper's boutique."

I wave my finger in the air. "Nuh-uh, I haven't decided yet. I'm never going to hear the end of this, am I?"

After seeing Connor at camp yesterday, Ford and I picked up some takeout from Catch 22, the restaurant on the water, then we went home and watched a movie before heading to bed where he most definitely used his hands and fingers in ways that I can't even manage to say out loud.

The lingerie set that Piper gave me is elegant and deserving of a big reveal, not an afterthought between rounds, therefore I'm reserving it for a special occasion.

"Suspense is your play, I respect that. It just means you envision a very long timeline for us; I do hope you realize that." He smirks to himself.

"I might."

This morning, I arrived downstairs, and Ford was closing a cooler, telling me not to worry about packing the picnic. I'd be lying if I said I don't have butterflies in my stomach.

I haven't been back to this lagoon since, well, before Connor.

"How do you know the lagoon isn't covered in garbage or the trees are gone. Maybe we are hyping this up," I think out loud.

"It's there." Ford is sure of himself.

"You've been back?"

"Once or twice. I would drive by with the boat, never went in, though."

God, is this what the past has done to us? We can't let go of places?

I look along the horizon to the right and see the opening to the spot that is responsible for holding our hearts captive. The trees hang over the passage. Willow trees, to be exact; the tree that blows tears in the wind.

Ford slows the boat down as we approach, and I get up off my seat to take a few steps to Ford, standing by his side and holding his arm before we both duck under the weeping tree as we enter.

We found this place one day when we decided to venture

off from our group who were partying on the shore nearby. It became our spot, our refuge.

And luckily, now I can witness that it hasn't changed. It's still quiet and beautiful. Calm lake water with a small little beach, perfect for two.

Ford turns the engine off and throws the rope to the sand. He hops over the edge, with the water to his knees. After he ties the rope to a tree trunk, he returns to the boat to offer me his hand.

"Come on."

Our eyes connect, and everything feels slightly overpowering but in the best possible way.

When I'm about to hop into the water, Ford grabs me in a manner that enables him to carry me and ensure I stay dry.

"What service," I joke.

"For you, I'd crawl on my knees."

I laugh before my feet land on dry earth. We take a few moments to lay out a big blanket and set down the cooler. It isn't long until we are both lying down on propped elbows as we stare at the view.

"Here we are," I announce.

Ford interlaces our fingers on the blanket. "It's good to be back."

"It feels kind of coming full circle," I admit.

Glancing to my side, I see that Ford is ignoring the beautiful nature around us, as his focus is on me.

"It was our own little world."

I snort a laugh. "Oh, I know. Nobody ever came here, except that one time when a fisherman stopped, but then he saw us making out and left."

"Yeah, I remember that," he reflects with a grin of fondness.

"I'm confident this is where I got pregnant."

Ford moves to his side, and his fingers begin to play with the tie on my wrap. "Maybe."

"It was my fault."

He wastes no time to set his fingers on my jaw to guide my gaze to him. "No, it's not."

"I missed a pill."

"So? People take all their pills and still get pregnant. Besides, we have a great kid."

"I love him, but it could have been easier for us," I state.

Ford shakes his head. "We'll never know, and it doesn't matter. Here we are."

My lips roll in, and I can't think of how to articulate the array of emotions stirring inside of me. Something about this place, remembering younger me, the times we would lie here staring at the blue sky and talk about our dreams. We had crazy ideas that being together could be so easy. We'd get a place together, and I'd study law wherever Ford went. I wanted that because a textbook can be read anywhere, and Ford was the one and only.

Looking back, I see how he put me first. Letting go of my dreams wasn't an option to him, which is why he didn't fight our parents when we made the decision to keep Connor.

But damn, we were tormenting ourselves for years.

"I don't want my heart to break again," I whisper softly.

Ford leans down to brush the corner of my mouth with his lips. "It can't break." He is adamant and his voice rasps.

"I think it can."

He gently shakes his head no. "It never broke. I've just been holding onto it for a while, waiting for you to come back."

My heart swells at his words, and I tip my chin up to offer my mouth to him for a kiss. His lips press a firm kiss against my mouth, and I want to get lost in him. I slide my leg up his body until I snake around his waist, pulling him to me.

I murmur into his mouth, certain that everything inside of me has surrendered. My mind gave into his idea of having a week to ourselves, a selfish decision, but in truth, my heart already committed to more than a week long ago.

"I'm scared." Our mouths can't part. It's a constant back and forth of our lips sealing together, attempting to get air, only to return like a magnet. "Of this."

"Tell me." Ford showers me with kisses. "What has you scared?"

I manage to escape his hold and scoot up to sitting, well aware my wrap is twisted and halfway off my body. "We're in the grasp of having it all. It's possible, right?"

Ford flashes me a smile of comfort. "I believe so."

"I can't be responsible around you. We are unable to go slow, with our relationship, I mean." I dip my head down and attempt to hide my happiness from that fact.

Ford tucks my braid behind my shoulder. "I think ten years has been slow enough, don't you?"

"Yeah."

"Listen, soon Connor is back home. *Our* home. I know we need to be sensitive around him, but he isn't a small kid anymore."

"Oh, I noticed." I breathe a sigh.

Ford leads me back to lying. "Let's just take it one step at a time… to our final destination."

"Which is?" I squint my eyes at him.

He scoffs a sexy laugh before nuzzling his nose against my hair. "That ring deserves to be around your finger."

I pretend to be shocked. "What intentions."

Ford tickles me in response, and we both get tangled in

one another until we realize we are at the moment where real entwines with dreams.

"I never stopped loving you, Elle."

I wrap my arms tighter around his neck. "I love you too, but I guess you knew that since you had my heart this whole time."

"Damn straight."

His hand moves between us to untie my wrap, and my body is already aching. Ford groans as his mouth clasps onto my nipple through my bikini.

I moan and bite my lower lip. "You're trouble. Not even thirty minutes in and we are adding public indecency to our day."

"You didn't seem to mind ten years ago," Ford reminds me before he lowers the fabric.

My nipple is a prisoner between his teeth, and I hiss in pleasure. "Didn't Lake Spark become more of a tourist destination since then? Are we really alone?"

He peers up from his efforts. "It's just you, me, and the sky."

My clit pulses from the need I have for this man to be inside of me. "Then do things to me that will make the sky wish it could hide." I notice my tone is more sultry than normal.

Ford chuckles deep in the back of his throat before he makes a point to ensure I watch him as his fingers disappear under the bottom of my bikini, his touch launching instant fireworks inside of my body.

"My fingers are already soaking." Ford's voice is thick with approval and heat.

Feeling his fingers slide in a line then circle, I hood my lids closed and sink into his connection. "What can I say? I'm craving your touch."

He brings his finger up to my lips, and I open to suck, knowing he likes to watch me taste myself. Needing more, I rub against his body, feeling his solid length against my stomach.

His finger pops out of my mouth and is replaced by Ford's warm hungry kiss that shoots desire down my spine.

"Roll to your side," he whispers his demand into my ear, causing my sensitive parts to tingle.

Obeying, I roll away from him, and I feel his hand lower his swim trunks just enough before he unties half of my bikini bottoms to give room, and his tip swirls along my pussy, dragging my arousal around until he aligns and enters me with ease.

As I look over my shoulder, he meets my mouth to swallow my moans as he moves inside of me while his hand travels from holding my hip in place, along my oblique, before sneaking up to tweak my nipples.

I gasp from the overload of sensations.

"You feel too good," Ford mumbles against my skin.

Deep inside, I feel him reach a part of me that's the button to awakening extreme pleasure that he can deliver on every move.

"Good thing you don't plan on letting me go," I murmur. I reach my arm behind me to hook around his neck, causing my body to elongate and offer a better canvas to Ford.

The sound of our skin slapping is the only sign that we're not going slow. I'm so lost in Ford that our rhythm is irrelevant because every thrust is heavenly.

"I can't get enough of this."

My breath grows heavy. "Me too."

His finger travels down to my clit, and I'm happy we are lying down because my entire body feels like it's floating, only being grounded by Ford's touch.

Kissing him is my secret weapon for stability. He leads us and keeps me from falling, because I'm about to explode, and he knows it too.

"I want you coming around my cock," he demands into my ear while his finger circles my clit.

"Only if you promise to come."

He laughs sinisterly causing a tickle below my ear. "Baby, I'm only satisfied if you come and then I fill you up."

I nod and close my eyes as my senses heighten, and a few more strokes and I'm almost there.

"That's it," he coos.

Ford thrusts harder, and a wave travels below my navel, flowing until I'm pulsing and shaking around him.

My body goes completely spent and into a state of utter bliss as he continues to move.

It's when his head falls against my shoulder and I feel him still that I know Ford joined me on the satisfaction scale.

He stays inside of me, and that's what I love the most about the last few days, just being completely dissolved into one another, truly one.

I hum a sound to express my current state as Ford places a kiss on my shoulder.

"I feel like my thighs might be shaking for days," I tell him.

"Excellent." He tucks his head into the curve at the base of my neck. "One day we'll come back here and we'll make another baby."

Instantly, I stutter out a sound. "You're crazy."

"No, I'm not."

"You make me feel like you're completely enamored with me."

I feel a loss the moment he slides out of me to drag his shorts back up. "Solid observation."

I roll my eyes as I wiggle to retie my bikini. Ford is quick to help me with the strings around my neck.

Now covered, I move to sit between his legs, with my back to his stomach and his arms finding a home around me.

"I hope you put on sunscreen; the sun is strong today."

He kisses the top of my head. "Remember that time we came out here and we forgot? You looked like a lobster for days."

I laugh at the memory. "Yeah, and I was red everywhere, not one inch spared; bikini lines gone, which meant everyone knew I had been naked."

"With me." He grins with pride.

"Exactly."

"Do you know what I think is amazing?"

I kiss his upper arm that rests across my shoulder. "What?"

"Even when we weren't together, I'm the lucky guy who knew you from the beginning. We have a history. I'm your first, and I know every little thing about you. We share a child, connected for life. Nobody could come close to that; I get to be the one who sees you in a different light."

My tongue runs a line inside my mouth. "I know the feeling. You are my rock, even when I chose not to admit it."

"I promise I won't sink you down." He squeezes me tighter.

"Nah, it's okay, you can. Everything inside of me felt weighted down before. Every time I thought any chance of us would go out the window, I couldn't move on. Now, I know I felt that way because you're worth the wait. We were always going to find our way back, I believe that now."

"Is it possible to feel so incredibly happy that you know it makes up for lost time?"

My shoulders come up to my ears in doubt. "I guess we'll find out."

"Yeah, we will."

Over the next hour or two, we swim and have some drinks from the cooler. As I watch Ford load the boat, I can't seem to shake this feeling that, as much as we trust our change in relationship, we are currently in our own world and bubble.

What happens when the outside world sticks a pin in it?

FORD

Connor drops his bag by the door to the garage and starts to run in the direction of the den off the main living room that houses the game system. Today was the end of camp.

"Hey, cutie, how about we pick up the bag you left on the floor?" Brielle suggests with a sweet smile as she walks from the kitchen, drying her hands with a towel.

I was on pick-up duty, as I wanted to check a few things in my office, and Brielle stayed home to study in quiet.

Our son groans and mopes back on the trail he took until he picks up the backpack, then hangs it on the hook. "Happy now?"

"Very," Brielle answers dryly.

Connor starts his trek, but I grab him by the back of his shirt. "Whoa there, cowboy, how about a hug for your mom?"

"Ugh, fine." Connor walks to his mom and gives her a lazy hug.

"How about I get you a snack?" Brielle ignores his behavior and coddles him.

"I'm starving. Can I have popcorn?" he asks.

"Sure."

Then he is off again.

I rub my face, reminding myself that he's a kid who is entering an awkward age because these sure as hell are no longer the days of never leaving our sides because Mom and Dad are the best thing in the whole world. Following Brielle back into the kitchen, she heads straight to the cupboard to collect a popcorn bag.

"He needs to unwind, but after that, it's full-on family time whether he likes it or not." I grab vitamin water from the fridge.

Brielle is busy pressing buttons on the microwave. "You're right." She turns and heads to the sink to clean a mug she must have used while I was away.

Walking straight to her, I stand behind her and allow my hand to sneak underneath her skirt to tease that soft stretch of skin on her inner thigh.

She gasps instantly. "What are you doing?" she mutters, and I can hear her smile.

"It's impossible not to touch you when the opportunity arises."

"Ford, our son is in the other room, and you better get used to behaving because we're not sharing a bed the next few nights."

I sigh at the reminder, but this morning we agreed that it was for the best. Connor is the priority, and we need to be tactful and slowly ease him into the change in his parents' relationship status.

Ignoring the reality of our parameters, I let us have these few minutes while our son is nowhere in sight. I slip my finger between her thighs, riding up but stopping short, but it doesn't mean I don't feel her heat near my finger. I bet if I touched her pussy, she would be soaking, but I'm not that reckless.

My other hand grabs her hair with a little force to bring her neck to my mouth. "All I want to do is watch you touch yourself to show me how much you want me before I bend you over the kitchen counter and defile you until you scream," I growl low against her throat.

"That's quite a picture you paint," she hisses.

"I'm not the teenage boy you lost your virginity to. I'm a man now who has had years to think of all the dirty things I want to do to you, before I kiss you gently because I love you."

I pull her tight to me, only to feel her shudder as she melts against my body.

"Ford," she hums.

"Why don't we take these off?" I begin to tug on the string of her thong.

A scoffed sound escapes her mouth which now hangs open. "No way. You need to back up and find me a bowl for the popcorn." She shimmies against me but rides my finger at the same time as the sound of corn kernels popping fills the room.

"I can get used to you standing in my kitchen." I move my hand away from her middle and follow the curve of her ass that I gently spank before stepping back. "A bowl you said?" I casually inquire, as if nothing just happened.

Brielle grips the edge of the sink as she catches her breath. "Yeah, and some manners!" She twists her body and playfully swats me as I walk away.

Grabbing a ceramic bowl from the shelf, I proceed to open the microwave that beeped.

"Should we do homemade pizzas for dinner? That's easy, right?" She seems to be focused again.

I wash my hands then pour the bag of corn into the bowl. "Sounds good. Tomorrow, we can just chill by the pool, or go on the boat, walk around town. I kind of feel like Pioneer Park is no longer on the list of options."

Our son rejoins the room and is quick to inform us, "No way. I'm way too old for that shit."

"Whoa, language." I'm not impressed and hold the bowl up in the air so he can't reach it. "Maybe we keep that word out of our vocabulary."

"Why? Other kids and Aunt Violet say it all the time." He attempts to reach for the popcorn.

"You are not other kids, and Aunt Violet is in her twenties, trying to figure out her life, and she still considers ice cream its own food group, so she's not exactly the pillar of goals."

I notice Brielle drop her face into her palm. "How about we try a clean slate from your arrival at home."

Connor sits on a stool and slouches against the counter. "Sure, but it's Dad's home, not yours."

Brielle's jaw clenches, and I can tell she is frustrated with the attitude.

I carelessly drop the bowl of popcorn onto the counter, ready to correct him. "It's family week. My home is your home, it's your mother's home, it's our home. Clear? Got it? Great."

His hand claws the snack. "Fine. Is this all because I told my teacher that you two act strange sometimes?"

Brielle steps closer to the counter. "It's because we should do more things as a family. We don't always need to keep everything to your time with Dad or your time with me."

"I get it. You want to do things together outside of special occasions."

"Bingo." Brielle taps her finger into the air.

Our son now has a mouth full of popcorn. "What's for dinner? I'm starving."

"You're eating right now." Brielle looks on in astonishment.

"I know, but I've worked up an appetite. I built muscle the last two weeks." He proudly flexes his arm.

Brielle and I look at one another and smile. "You're a growing boy."

"A little man," I add.

He chomps on more popcorn. "Exactly."

"I guess I will get to work on pizza then." Brielle walks to the fridge, and I continue to lean against the counter, staring at Connor who is oblivious that he has it so lucky; everything we do is for him.

———

APPARENTLY, food is the key to Connor's growing attitude. His mood pepped up after a second slice of pizza. Brielle made everyone their own, which is perfect since we all have different tastes. We're sitting outside on the patio around the pool relaxing and being together, just the three of us.

For the most part, we've always had a reason to be together for dinners. A birthday, a school recital, or a postgame dinner. We never did this just because... and it feels too right.

"The dog is here," Connor points out.

We all skim our gaze in his line of sight and see April and Spencer's beagle, Pickles, padding along into our yard. It happens occasionally. He is harmless and old, except when he sees Spencer or a squirrel, then suddenly, he has puppy energy.

"Ah, we will need to take him back. Most of the time,

April doesn't realize he wandered off. I'm pretty certain a raccoon or something will get to him one of these days."

"Ford," Brielle scolds me.

I roll my shoulder back before picking up my beer bottle. "What? It's true. This is Lake Spark."

"Can I have a dog?" Connor asks before taking a bite of his food.

"Since when do you want a dog?" Brielle grabs the salad bowl.

"I'm a kid, shouldn't I have a phase of wanting a dog?"

I chuckle at his reply. "You're a kid now? A few hours ago, you made it clear you're no longer a kid."

"Stop with the psychology," my son retorts.

"A dog is a lot of responsibility," Brielle notes as she watches Pickles walk to me for a pat on his head.

"True, and soon I will have hockey practice like all of the time," he explains.

I rub my chin, as I can only imagine Connor in a few years playing high school hockey. There is a prep school nearby with a great team.

"How about you take Pickles back after dinner? That's the closest you can get to having a dog," Brielle suggests.

"No way. Hadley is there, and she looks at me all funny."

I grin to myself. "Hadley is younger than you, probably with a little crush, and I'm not sure she's there since Spencer has an away game this week, so April was going to take her to watch."

"Exactly, it's yuck that she has a crush on me."

Brielle reaches to her side to touch Connor's arm with affection. "It's not yuck. It just means you are a handsome guy. And get used to it, because as you get older, then, well, I hate to tell ya, but the girls will be lining up."

"Can we end this conversation? Next thing I know, you

will be giving me the baby talk and how it has to happen later in life. Aunt Violet says you two are the exception and made me early, and you won't let me forget it so I won't become a dad in a few years."

Brielle gives me wide eyes, with a look that is half-worried and half-entertained.

"Your Aunt Violet, to my surprise, makes a solid point." Huh, my sister kind of nailed it. I tip my beer back for a sip.

"Tomorrow, can we just hang by the pool?" Connor drops his pizza on the plate.

Brielle nods. "Sounds good. I can study."

"That big test," he volleys.

"Exactly," she says. "I have a really big test to take. Two days of tests, which is why you might spend a little extra time with your dad this summer," Brielle explains.

I notice Pickles is resting at my feet. Hopefully, he doesn't get too comfortable. "We'll hold down the fort, and when your mom finishes her test, then we can celebrate."

"Does that mean we are going to the jewelry store?" Connor innocently asks, but Brielle chokes on her drink.

She attempts to clear her throat. "Why do you say that?" Her voice is strained.

Our son looks at her. "Because that's what we always do when it's a special occasion. Geez, Mom, you know nobody at this table believes in Santa, so who do you think helped me pick out your Christmas necklace?"

A wry smile is now permanent on my lips, especially when I notice Brielle look down at the necklace she is playing with, the necklace from Connor.

"I mean, I assumed you had some help," she says in an attempt to defuse this conversation.

I scratch my cheek. "How about you drop Pickles off, Connor? I'll grab the ice cream from the freezer," I suggest.

Connor stands up, and Pickles' head perks up. "Come on, my parents are trying to get rid of me so they can whisper about me because they think I'm clueless."

Hot damn, even I'm stuck on how to respond, and when I look at Brielle still with a frozen smile, then I know that I'm not alone.

Watching Connor walk away with the dog in tow, Brielle and I sigh a heavy breath of relief that we got away without addressing his comment.

"What do you think he meant?" I wonder.

"I don't know, but that was my cue to open the wine." She laughs.

Since I am ever the gentleman, I stand up to lean across the table to grab a bottle of white and pop the cork for her with an opener.

As I twist the top, I glance up to notice that Brielle is staring at me with deep fondness. "Yes?" I draw it out.

She holds up her glass, ready for me to pour the vino. "His remark about Christmas jewelry, it just has me thinking."

"About?"

Probably the way that I used our son to ensure you wear a piece of me.

"He's right. Santa didn't help him buy expensive jewelry, and that if it hadn't been a gift from him then I would have been adamant you returned it. Do you know what I think?"

I tip the bottle over her glass. "Go on."

"We sometimes used our son to be together in some way."

My jaw flexes side to side, as she caught me out. "You know it's true."

"You put in a lot of thought with gifts."

"It was my responsibility to guarantee that he bought you

gifts for your birthday, Christmas, and Mother's Day," I say, brushing it off.

She takes a decent sip of wine. "And I'm the one who maybe enjoys the fact that I know you had a hand in picking out this very expensive, beautiful, and perfect necklace with a little boat on it, which I'm certain Connor has no idea what it means."

I don't flinch, instead soaking in the truth of her theory. Walking around the table, I lean down and touch her chin to bring her lips up, and I capture her mouth for a kiss. "You are so incredibly smart. I have no doubt you will pass the Bar. Then maybe I can give you a gift without using Connor as the middleman."

"I don't want gifts. I want you." Her voice is raspy, and her smile never fades.

Recementing our lips, I take more, maybe I'm even greedy, and she murmurs as our breaths mingle.

"I swear, Elle, after he goes to bed, I'm finding a way to make love to you," I speak against her lips.

Brielle giggles and sinks back in her chair. "I think my beautiful glistening pussy needs a rest from your cock."

My mouth drops open in shock. "Your mouth!"

"What?"

"I've never heard you use such language. It's…" I don't know what it is. She is so prim and proper, yet she has just blown my mind. Do I like her like this? It's a surprise. Maybe I get my kicks out of her acting innocent half the time. I think about it for a few seconds. "Fucking hot."

She shoos me away with her hand, but I ignore her and dive in for one more kiss, only to quickly step back when we hear footsteps.

"Nobody is home, so I put Pickles behind the gate."

I swipe my hand through my hair as I see Connor in the

corner of my eye. "Hey, kiddo. Sorry, I still need to grab the ice cream."

He walks back to his seat at the table.

"I'm not an idiot, Dad, I know this whole family-time story is so that you can both tell me that you're changing custody or someone is moving to someplace else, something like that."

Oh shit, we need to rectify this.

"Hey, no, wait, why would you think that? If anything, we'll be doing more things together."

Brielle is quick to jump in. "Exactly. Nobody is moving or changing custody, just more together time. That's great, right?"

Connor looks between us, skeptical. "Oh."

I blow out a breath and rest my hands behind my head. "You okay? Is that what you have been thinking this is?"

"I mean, you're both always awkward around one another, but today you both seem extra... I don't know, like you're happy and gearing me up for something."

Brielle taps her wine glass and nods her head in under-standing. "You can relax, really," she promises.

"Okay, cool."

"I'll grab the ice cream." I begin to walk in the direction of the house but stall. "Connor, you don't see it as a bad thing that we're all together the next few days, right? I mean, now that you know nothing bad is happening."

He shrugs his shoulder. "I guess, it still sucks being the only child, though."

My eyes grow big. "Just add it to your never-ending wish list, okay, kiddo?"

Brielle snorts a cute little laugh.

And as I walk into the house, I feel like we may just be lucky, and easing him into our new dynamic might be a breeze. But I also wonder why he never asked if we were getting back together. It doesn't even seem to be a thought in his brain.

I realize that not many things in life make me nervous. I do well under pressure; how else was I a star hockey player? Yet telling Connor about his mom and me? It has me anxious.

Maybe I won't get the father-of-the-year award, but I think tomorrow we rip the band-aid off, because I'm sure as hell not sneaking around.

FORD

W alking into my home office, I pause when I take in the mass of post-it notes, highlighters, and notebooks splayed across my desk. My head tilts to the side as I wait for Brielle to look up at me, or at least notice that I'm here, as she is immersed in her book.

Clearing my throat, I wiggle my fingers at my side and my eyes circle the room, taking in the morning light.

"Morning," she says as she finishes writing a note before slamming the pen down and offering me a gorgeous smile.

I approach the desk, happy that she is making herself at home. "What time did you get up?"

"I think six." She doesn't seem sure. "Wanted to get a study session in."

I perch on the edge of my desk and dip my head down to kiss her. Would have preferred if I woke to her in my bed, but Connor is back, and clearly, Brielle has a few things on her mind.

She hums as I kiss her deeper, and I wish I didn't have to pull away. "I think you need a break."

"Oh yeah?" she whispers before her tongue delves into my mouth and her fingers curl around the fabric of my shirt.

I touch her wrists to steady us. As much as I have a few scenarios for this room, we need to talk.

Reluctantly pulling away, I give her one more quick chaste kiss before holding her hands on my lap. "How about we do a pool session this morning, then I take Connor into town so you can have a little space to study?" I suggest.

"Sounds good. Is he up already?" she wonders.

"I heard him stirring when I came down the stairs."

"I should go make him some breakfast." Brielle begins to get up, but I'm quick to hold her wrist to prevent her from getting far, and she gives me a bewildered look.

"He knows how to use a bowl and spoon. One morning of Coco Puffs isn't going to kill him. He's fine," I assure her because I know she insists he eats a big healthy breakfast every morning, often including her slaving over the griddle to make him pancakes.

She smirks to herself. "I guess you're right."

"Relax, okay?" She nods in agreement. "So, I was thinking while I'm with Connor that maybe he and I could have a little talk. Man to man, you know?"

"What do you mean?" She seems a little curious and concerned.

I run my hand along her arm to ease her. "I know we have a lot to discuss, but I think he's old enough that we don't need to be so delicate around him. He's smart."

She sighs and sinks back into the chair. "Shouldn't we tell him together? Wait a little, too? I mean, we're so fresh."

"We've been together for ten years, just not in a physical sense. I think you can agree."

Her nose raises slightly. "After I sit for the Bar, then we

can tell Connor and drop the bombshell to our parents, figure out how to make this work."

"We'll work." My tone is a little sharp. "We will do all of that, but Connor is different, and I think sneaking around him only elevates stress levels."

"Maybe." She breathes out. I notice she is biting the inside of her cheek. "Don't you want to tell him together?"

"I think it's a talk that he and I need to have. Can you trust me on this?"

Her eyes meet mine and are filled with faith and contentment. "Okay. Tell him."

A soft smile spreads on both our faces. This time when she stands, I follow her lead and wrap my arms around her middle to kiss her one more time.

I mutter against her lips. "It will be fine."

She nuzzles her nose against my cheek, and I can tell that she inhales my scent. "I hope so."

Me too.

————

CONNOR and I walk down Main Street with ice cream cones in hand. We go slow to avoid our cones turning into a mess of melting ice cream. I motion to the bench up ahead that overlooks the park and gazebo by the lake.

"Mom is going to be upset that she missed ice cream from Jolly Joe's," he comments before taking another lick from his chocolate ice cream.

I swallow and take this as my moment. "It's okay, we'll get her a Turtle sundae to-go after we hit up the general store to grab a few things, as I want to BBQ tonight."

"You remember her favorite ice cream?"

I give my son a strange look. "I've known her longer than you have. Of course I know."

"She'll be happy if we bring her back ice cream."

We both sit down.

"Exactly. Your mom really needs us to make her life a little easier the coming weeks," I begin. "Her test is something she has been working for her whole life."

"She would be a lawyer already if it wasn't for me."

I toss the small remnants of my cone into the garbage not far from us and lean against the back of the bench, examining him, trying to figure out if his comment was an observation with thought behind it or not. "It's a bit more complicated than that. She wanted to spend more time with you when you were younger."

My son doesn't look up from his ice cream cone. "Yeah, because you were always away for games and training."

His words hit me hard, and a twinge of pain flutters across my chest. "Is that what you think?" Connor rolls his shoulder back. "We were young, and hockey was a way I could give you a life with anything you could ask for."

"I know, you guys tell me all the time."

My jaw clenches as I debate where to take our conversation. "Connor, I'm not going to talk to you like a little boy because you've made it clear the last few days that you are no longer one. So here we are, father and son, man to man, and I want to be honest with you."

"About what?" he asks, oblivious and focusing on his ice cream.

Bringing my hand to his shoulder, I decide to dive into the deep end. "Your mom. Me. Your mom and I." His eyes instantly blaze with curiosity. "I know we've raised you where your mom and I are friends, nothing more, but the truth is, we don't want that. We're together again."

"What do you mean?" His eyes turn strange.

"That your mom and I are in a relationship together. I'm telling you because we don't want to hide it from you."

"Why isn't she here?"

"Because I felt you and I needed to talk. I've noticed you have more observations and opinions lately, lucky us." I attempt to offer him a soothing smile. "Us together is new, but the feelings we have for each other have always been there. We just focused on other things."

"Like me."

"Yeah, and other goals. Truthfully, I've wanted to be with your mom for a long time, but it took the moment where we seem to have achieved all of those goals for me to go after the one thing that should have been my priority all along."

My son looks up at me with something that I can only pinpoint as a sensitive understanding or attempting to grasp my words. Gone is the child I carried on my shoulders and helped when he fell the first time on the ice. Here is a man in the making.

"Is it why Mom sometimes seemed sad after you would visit?"

I'm cracking inside from the reminders of the facts I already knew. Hearing it from him feels like a heavier punch, one that even reality couldn't throw at me. "Probably. But I have every intention of ensuring she is never sad another moment in her life."

Connor raises his chin slightly, as if he's sizing me up. "Is this really happening? I mean, you're both not going to change your minds, are you?"

I scratch my chin, proud that he is protective of his mother, the way he should be. "I don't think so. In fact, one day I hope to marry your mom. It's like this, Connor, everything was already there, every little amazing part that you need to make a relationship that lasts forever, except there was one missing piece, but now we decided to take that piece and add it to our lives."

"What's the part that was missing?"

I laugh and gently nudge his shoulder. "Well, I think you noticed we weren't romantic with one another. That's no longer the case. I want to kiss your mom all the time."

"TMI, Dad." He looks at me with funny disgust that is all in good fun. "Does this mean we are going to live together?"

"Can you do me one favor?" He nods. "We will talk about where we will live, school, dog or no dog, and what this all means for our family *after* your mom sits her exam in a few weeks. Right now, she needs us as her cheerleaders, and questions come later."

"Right, I can do that."

I smile. "Good. Now, tell me, how do you feel about all of this?"

Connor takes a moment and eats the last of his ice cream, making a point to drag this out because my boy got my streak of humor and games.

"I think…" he begins, "this is the best news." A smile spreads on his face.

Placing my hand on his shoulder, my face is elated. "I was hoping you would say that."

"What if I said I didn't like it?"

"Connor, as much as we do everything for you because you are our number one, sometimes your parents get to put themselves first, and then it would have been our job to prove to you that we are the real thing, and we make one another happy."

"This news is kind of cool."

We look at one another with an understanding that I'm proud to have with him. It's the type of dynamic that I missed with my own folks. Maybe that is why Brielle and I are so damn good at parenting; we learned what we needed to do better. And here I am in an honest and open conversation with my son, listening and being patient.

The thought of my parents brings a near scowl to my face. "Listen, I know you talk to Gramps and your grandparents via text sometimes. But let's wait to tell them the news, okay? We'll save everything for a few weeks from now."

"Uh-huh. Now is stress-free time for Mom, so just the pool, ice cream, and kissing at dinner when you think I'm not looking," he lists.

He grabs my attention as my head perks at his words, and I connect a few dots. He moves to throw away his napkin, but he doesn't get far because I gently take hold of the back of his shirt.

"You saw us last night, didn't you?" I have to grin.

He shrugs his shoulders. "Maybe."

"That's a yes. Were you going to bring it up or..." I wonder.

A cheeky smile spreads on his mouth. "You told me we were going for ice cream, just you and me. Everyone knows that means a talk is coming. It's a classic parent move."

"So, you let me sweat it out for a little?"

"For sure, Aunt Violet said I should too when I texted her."

I laugh because this is an unexpected turn, and I find humor in it. My sister means well, and I like that she is a sounding board for him, so I'm not mad.

"Anything else?"

Connor shakes his head. "Nah, I'll save the sibling talk for later."

"Yeah, you and me both, kid. Come on, we need to go to

the store and get home to Mom." I stand and wait until he is off the bench.

We begin to walk back to Main Street, and I'm relieved that we can finally focus on being the family we always wanted.

BRIELLE

Ripping up pieces of lettuce, I occasionally glance at my phone. Lena is on the other end of our video call, soaking in all the details of my whirlwind few days. Her jaw dropped two sentences in, and I think she is still trying to wrap her head around it.

I probably should be too, but it all feels right. "I know it's crazy, but I feel like Ford maybe has a point and this is now our time."

Lena closes her mouth, and her head moves in different angles as she tries to form a sentence. "It's fast. However, I guess… it's no different to before, just now you upgraded to some serious benefits. I mean, you two were always emotionally there for one another, protective of each other, and now you can openly admit what you've been toeing around, plus add the physical aspect. It's not like you two are strangers. You talk on a daily basis… and have been for ten years."

I grab my half-filled wine glass to sip my Chardonnay. "Exactly, right? I'm not being irresponsible, am I?" Should I have more doubts?

Lena shakes her head. "Ford? He would kill for you, so

no; he would never hurt you. Maybe being *together* together is different now that you're older?" Her voice grows squeaky, as even Lena isn't sure what to question. "Nah, it goes back to what I just said, you've both kind of been in a relationship, emotionally unavailable to anyone else, so if the physical aspect feels stellar, then I think you're good to go."

"Absolutely no complaints in that department." I try to keep my face serious, but I can't control the satisfied smirk that wants to break out. It causes Lena to clap like a penguin in excitement for me. "Anyhow, I'll be staying here for a few more days, then I need to head back to Hollows. My study group is meeting up again almost every day until the exams."

"I'm sure Ford can destress you a few times." She couldn't help herself and teases me.

I gulp a sip of wine. "Unfortunately, he is staying in Lake Spark and is going to keep Connor here so I can have some quiet."

Her face softens. "He wants this for you as much as you do."

"I think so. I'm curious how the man-to-man talk went. I think Connor wants us together. What kid doesn't want their parents together?"

She shrugs. "You'd be surprised, families come in different shapes. I'm just happy for you."

"Thanks. I should go, they'll be home any minute."

We both say our goodbyes, and I look down at the bowl of salad that is now home to tiny pieces of shredded lettuce because I got carried away daydreaming while prepping the salad.

Ignoring it, I grab the cucumber and begin to cube the vegetable with a knife. Randomly, I begin to wonder if a cucumber is really a fruit. I'm in doubt now and hold the green thing in the air to examine it.

I nearly drop it when I'm startled to feel two hands sneak up and snake around me, squeezing.

"Don't worry, there is no comparison," Ford informs me from behind.

Rolling my eyes, I lean back as he wraps his arms around me, enjoying being this way with him. "Is cucumber a vegetable?"

"I have no clue."

"It's a fruit," our son announces as he walks into the kitchen.

Instantly, from habit, I attempt to get Ford to back up, but he doesn't give in.

Instead, he leans down to whisper in my ear. "He knows."

Turning quickly in Ford's arms, my eyes grow big. "And?" I whisper back.

"Why don't you ask him?" Ford says in a normal tone with a neutral look, yet a hint of joy is there to ease me.

Stepping out of his hold, I walk into the middle of the kitchen with caution. "So, you and your dad talked?"

Our son doesn't look at me, instead putting something in the freezer before he searches the cupboards for what I can assume is food. "Yeah, no big deal."

"No big deal?" I'm slightly disappointed. I thought for sure this would be one of the greatest days of his life.

Connor turns to me with a box of Pop-Tarts in his hand.

I take the box from him because he will ruin his dinner. His glance down informs me he knows my logic. "Don't want to talk about it?"

"It's cool. Now you guys don't have to pretend everything is fine when it really wasn't."

My mouth opens but only a rambled sound escapes me. I feel Ford's presence behind me, and he rests his hands on my shoulders to send comfort through my blood.

"Connor means he is thrilled. If he's trying to make his mom freak out for fun, then he knows he needs to stop." Ford is speaking more to our son than me. "He saw us last night and didn't let me know until *after* our conversation," he grits out to me.

"Oh. You saw your dad and I…"

"Kissing. It's kind of gross but kind of sweet. Can we not make a big deal about it?" Connor pleads as he opens God knows what sports drink he just grabbed from the fridge that is fluorescent blue.

I pretend to zip my lips. "Not a word from me."

Ford clears his throat, and there is an odd tension in the room until Connor walks around the counter and comes to give me a hug. My ten-year-old is willingly giving me a hug, and I'm not going to waste a second questioning this. I bear-hug the heck out of him.

"Dad can really make you happy now."

I look down at my son who has a twinkle in his eye and a soft smile. I brush his hair back with my hand and cradle his head. "He can."

"I will," Ford corrects me.

"Is this all happening too fast?" I ask our son.

He shakes his head. "It makes life a hell of a lot easier."

"Language," Ford warns him, and I'm grateful that he is here to take the authoritative tone because I don't always want to be the rule mom.

"Sorry."

"I'm happy you're happy," I say.

He nods. "We brought you a Turtle sundae."

I smile brightly. "Is that what you placed in the freezer?"

"Yeah."

"The key to my heart," I reply.

Connor scoffs a sound and backs away. "Don't get sappy on us now."

"My mistake," I one-tone.

"I'm going to play a game now, Dad said I could before dinner."

"Thirty minutes, then I want you outside," Ford reminds him, but Connor is already turning the corner down the hallway.

I swivel on my toes to face the man who made this transition somewhat easy for me.

"What did you say?" I'm far too curious and loop my arms around Ford's neck.

He plays it cool. "Not much. Sometimes the obvious doesn't need to be explained."

Ford kisses my cheek, leaving me there to reflect on his comment.

———

A LITTLE WHILE LATER, I'm walking barefoot out onto the patio where Ford is working the grill. I place my ridiculous bowl of chopped salad on the table. I can't help myself, I drink in the view of Ford. Something about late-afternoon sun hits him just right. He's extra sexy as he flips a burger, occasionally drinking from his beer. He has no clue that I'm admiring him, feeling lucky that he is someone that I get to call mine.

Music plays on the Bluetooth, "My Sweet Baby" by Thieving Birds. I like this song.

Ford glances up, catching me in my near-drooling state. He grins, sets the grill tongs down, and walks around the BBQ to me.

"You look relaxed," he comments.

"I am. It should be one of the most stressful times of my life, yet I feel almost Zen," I remark.

Ford steps to me, pulling me around the waist to his body, and he holds my hand in his when he begins to lead us in a sway. "See? I sometimes have good ideas."

"You mean to get me here under false pretenses and get us to admit what we want?"

"Absolute brilliance," he remarks.

He twirls me around with our bodies flush, but it's nothing compared to his eyes that hold me captive as the sun causes a glint in his eyes.

"It's all okay," he assures me.

"I'm beginning to believe that," I say softly. "Connor does seem fine. He is, right?"

"Totally. I did tell him the sibling request needs to be on hold."

I laugh. "Good, we have time."

Ford tilts me back. "Just tell me when we have the green light on that."

I playfully nudge his shoulder before returning to our embrace for a dance on the patio under the summer sky.

"You just focus on that Bar now, okay? Everything else is for later," he promises.

"Sounds good."

Ford's fingers slide along my cheek into my hair, and he gives me a warning glare before his mouth meets mine for a warm kiss that keeps me grounded to the earth because this man is like a foundation of a house, except it's my heart.

"Everything is ours for the taking," he murmurs against the corner of my mouth.

"It is." I kiss him again, and this time I bring my leg up around his waist as we sway in our dance, and my dress hikes slightly.

He growls as we both laugh, completely lost in our moment.

"You know, I think I can get away with sleeping in your room tonight," I inform Ford with a sultry tone.

"Thank fuck for miracles," he nearly groans before kissing me.

"Okay, lovebirds, don't burn my burger," Connor orders as he walks along the pool and straight into a chair.

Ford and I step back and study ourselves. Our clothes are ruffled and our lips swollen. Admittedly, we are proud of ourselves because we're happy.

And a few minutes later, we are all laughing around the table for dinner. It's a perfect setting.

———

SLIDING my phone to the other side of the counter, I decide to ignore it. My father sent a text checking in on my studying. As much as I know he means well, it also feels like pressure. I just quickly texted back that I had a study session this afternoon, which was true.

But now, I'm done for the day, and tomorrow I head back to my house, and because I am still at Ford's, then that means I get to join my guys right after I bring them a fresh bowl of snacks.

Filling a bowl with tortilla chips, I walk into the den off the hall to the laundry room. A complete man cave, and to my surprise, Ford and Connor are not gaming but watching television and laughing.

They ignore me as I wiggle my way between them on the sofa, offering my son the bowl first.

"What on earth are you two watching?" I look up to see dogs running an agility competition.

I feel Ford bring his arm around me on the back of the sofa, but his eyes stay fixed on the flat-screen on the wall.

"It's the national dog competition, they have to beat a certain time," my son explains.

"This is so ridiculous. This is on the sports channel, with the same guy who used to run commentary on my hockey games." Ford shakes his head in disbelief. "He actually looks serious. It's canines jumping over a pole, how is this earth-shattering?"

I listen in, and when the commentator says, *"Look at that border collie in his perfection, running the weevils, perfect form for his category,"* I snort a laugh, because it does sound ridiculous, so damn serious.

"You've been watching this all afternoon?" I wonder.

"Made him read his book first." Ford gives me side-eye with a proud smirk.

I sneak my hand behind Ford to urge him forward slightly and rub a circle on his back in appreciation, as I may have mentioned at breakfast today that we need to push the reading list a bit.

"Oh no." Ford throws his arms up in the air. "Totally a bad ending."

"That Irish setter was so much better," my son adds.

I glance between my guys. "You both are into this, like *really* into this."

"I mean, if you're going to name your dog Bullet, then you better deliver the score." Ford is still focused on the television.

"I hope they go back to dock jumping, that was awesome."

A half-laugh escapes me. "I'm not sure what I walked into, but I *think* you are the same people I saw at breakfast."

Connor glances back at me. "Can I have a drink?"

My eyes go wide. "You may have a drink, and you can get it yourself since you are fully capable."

He whines a sound but reluctantly gets up and heads to the kitchen.

I focus my attention on Ford, slipping my fingers underneath his t-shirt over his lower back, and a second later his gaze is on me.

"How was studying?"

"Okay. My dad texted, by the way."

Ford gives me a strained look. "He's going to be thrilled when he finds out about us."

I tickle his skin. "I think you kind of enjoy that." They've always had a civil enough relationship, the key word being *enough*.

He leans in to plant a kiss on my lips. "I may get a *little* satisfaction if I get to see his face when he finds out."

"Thought so." I grin.

"I'll run into town to pick up takeout from Catch 22. Mozzarella sticks for my lady?" he suggests.

My hands land on my heart. "I'm in love again."

He chuckles faintly, his hands finding my waist to slide me onto his lap. I take in this moment of pure serenity of the last few days.

Days. It causes my brain to run wild.

"Okay there?" Ford notices.

"We're not moving too fast, right? I mean, a few days in your bed and then here we are, already telling Connor that we are back together. We're not being irresponsible? It's just... it feels right."

A gentle smirk appears on his lips, and he tucks my hair behind my ear. "It is happening fast, but we've always been here. We've talked about this."

"I know. I just find myself in disbelief sometimes," I admit.

"Doubt?" I hear a tinge of fear in his voice.

"No way." I kiss his cheek. "Just trying to be a responsible human." I laugh.

"We are, don't worry. Now watch the Yorkie about to hop over a pole, it will be great for your mental health." He indicates with his head to the screen.

Connor groans as he reappears in the room with a bottle of juice. "Seriously, you two."

He flops onto the sofa, and we all evaluate each other. "Get used to it, my little prince," I inform him.

"Yeah, got the memo." There is a subtle smile on our son's face. "Yes, the frisbee competition is next." He seems to be lost again in the television.

"All stakes are on this round. This spaniel is the youngest in the competition, and if he wins, then this underdog will beat the odds," the commentator announces very seriously.

Examining Ford's face, and he can't keep it in. He loses it, laughing in hysterics. Then Connor follows, and the domino hits me.

We're together, hanging out on a normal day, a family.

Completely content.

The way it was meant to be.

Completely unaware that sometimes life decides to throw you something unexpected at the wrong time more than once.

BRIELLE

W alking into my hotel room, I sigh through my frown.

I'm exhausted, disappointed, and my stomach has been turning since late this morning. After weeks of preparation, I feel like it all went out the window.

Dropping my purse on the desk in the room, I attempt to smile at the flowers that Ford had delivered while I was at day one of my Bar exam yesterday. The last few weeks, I've studied my ass off, and I felt ready. I was always going to stay in a hotel near the test location so I wouldn't have to worry about the commute. Of course, Ford took that as his cue to upgrade my room to a suite in a fancy hotel.

The idea was that after I finished my last exam today, Ford would meet me here for a little celebration and an extra night just us in a hotel room. But I'm not in the mood to celebrate.

I've failed. I know I have.

Yesterday, I killed it and felt my answers were on point for every question that I had to write out. Today? It started with my stomach bothering me, before I struggled to focus. In the end, I just filled out the multiple-choice answers not to leave anything blank, but my head was half absent.

I run my fingers along the card tucked between the roses.

You've got this. I'm proud of you.
Love you, Ford.

P.S. Connor loves you too, but the flowers were my idea because I plan on doing a few things to you later ;)

The sound of a keycard swiping on the door alerts me that Ford must have arrived only a minute or so after me.

Looking up, I see him swing the door open, drop his bag, and offer me his arms wide. "There's my lawyer."

Something inside of me cracks, and I run to him as tears fill my eyes. I bury my face into his chest, and Ford freezes for only a second before his arms wrap around me, walking us back into the room. I hear him kick the door closed, and he tucks my head under his chin to instantly soothe me, with his hand stroking my hair, before he plants a soft kiss on the top of my head.

"Shh, what's going on?" His voice is soft as I weep in his arms, with the sound of his heart under my ear.

"I failed," I mumble against his shirt that now has tears making a mess of the fabric.

"No, you didn't."

I pull back and sniffle. "I did, I froze. I mean, I purposely didn't eat anywhere last night to avoid food poisoning, but my stomach started to feel weird, and then my head just went somewhere else."

"Hey." Ford attempts to catch my eyes with his. "Doesn't

mean you failed. You had a great day yesterday, and I'm sure it's just stress that has you thinking this way."

I shake my head sadly. "It's not. I didn't test well today, and without the minimum score, I fail."

"Shh." He pulls me back into a tight hug. "Don't think about it now. It's over."

"All of this work for nothing," I vent. "I didn't even get to finish the exam properly. I blanked, and my answers weren't even relevant."

"I'm sorry, I wish you didn't feel this way. Come on, let's lie down for a little bit." Ford takes my hand in his and guides me to the bed. He lies down, and I follow his move, and he invites me to rest my head against his chest. It takes not even a second before his hands coast over my arms to ease me.

I sniffle again and feel dizzy from the array of emotions swirling inside of me.

"There is nothing you can do now except wait for the facts. Try and take your mind off it."

"It's really hard," I say, my voice cracking. "I was so close, and now I'm still not there."

Ford kisses my forehead, and his hand adjusts my hip so I'm hooked over his middle. "You're still close. You can retake the exam."

I scoff. "Yeah, in February."

"Elle, it's going to be okay."

I muffle another cry and give up on talking about it. I don't *want* to talk about it.

"I guess we have nothing to celebrate." I hiccup through my cry.

Ford rolls me to my back, hovering over me with a burning gaze. "Everything will work out the way it needs to. Have faith in that."

I nibble my bottom lip. "Hopefully."

"I can think of other reasons to enjoy tonight together." His long finger sneaks inside the buttons of my dress to caress my skin.

"I'm happy you're here, I am. I had planned to surprise you on the bed with the lingerie from Piper's boutique, but you arrived to a hot mess instead." I must have mascara running, snot dripping from my nose, and my face is puffy for sure.

Ford trails kisses down my throat, taking every drop of sadness with him, his lips purposely following the path of my tears. "You're beautiful as always, and we can just order room service and watch a movie. You feel a little warm, to be honest." His hand starts to pat my forehead, checking for a temperature.

"Great, failed the bar and ruined our planned night of debauchery."

He chuckles under his breath, plants a quick kiss on my lips, and gets up off the bed. "By all means, explicitly tell me every detail of what you had planned, but let me run you a bath first."

"I like that ide—" I'm unable to finish my sentence as I feel the need to gag, and I sit up, only to confirm that I need to throw up.

I run to the bathroom and heave until my insides are emptied into the toilet. I don't even notice my surroundings the next few minutes or that Ford followed and sits on the floor next to me, holding my hair and rubbing my back.

Flushing the toilet, I hang off the seat, slumped on the floor.

"This is the least romantic night we could have planned," I groan.

"Elle, we've been here before. Remember? It was impossible to hide your pregnancy from your parents because of your morning sickness," he remembers with a gentle wry smile, then he studies me for a second. "We're not…"

"No, I'm not pregnant." I had my period last week.

"Okay, how about I get that bath going?"

I nod once, unable to move much more.

Fifteen minutes later, I'm in the tub with Ford. He washes my back with a sponge while I try to relax. The pain in my stomach has returned, but this time it feels stabbing.

"If today wasn't like this, then what would we have done?" I wonder.

Ford leans back in the tub, and I rest between his legs. "We would never leave the room. I would have taken my time with you before we only stopped to have dinner for energy. After I had you in a state where you couldn't move, we would talk about what comes next with us. I might have had a gift for you."

I interlace our fingers and marvel at how perfectly we fit together. "A gift?" I raise my brow.

"You still deserve it; I'll give it to you when we are dry and wrapped together under the blankets."

"Now I'm curious." Although I think it's probably jewelry, that's Ford's thing.

His other hand is underwater, and even feeling sick, the sensitivity of his fingertips gliding up my thigh combined with the water makes me aroused, and he isn't even trying. My legs part open, wanting more of his touch, but a wave of dizziness hits me, and my head falls back onto Ford's shoulder as I close my eyes.

"I hope I don't make you sick with my flu."

"I'd take it ten times over if it meant you feel better."

"So sweet," I tease. "This is kind of a challenge. Being in a bath with you, naked, and I can't do very dirty things to you."

"Dirty, you say?" He groans into my ear just as his hand travels up my thigh, getting dangerously close to my pussy.

"I would have let you *explore* tonight." My tone dances, and I wait for his filthy thoughts to take over.

His fingers dig into my thigh, holding on for dear life. "Fuck," he grits out. "Everywhere, huh?'

"Everywhere," I reiterate. "If you tell me what my gift is, then maybe I will tell you how I would have used my mouth."

"You have tricks, Elle." He's amused. "But I wouldn't have let you lead, and you know that." Ford's lips brush along my cheekbone. "I would let you suck me the way you enjoy but only while you sit on my face because I'm always starving for your pussy."

The bath, this flu, or Ford. One of them is the culprit for the extreme heat wave flowing through my veins.

To make matters worse… "I'd do it while you wear an upgraded ring that's burning a hole in my pocket," he adds.

Bingo. That's my gift.

I glance over my shoulder and see he is satisfied with breaking the news to me. "I haven't bothered you about it since you gave it back, but make no mistake, I haven't forgotten."

"That's a *big* discussion. But by all means, I should consider your proposition and standpoint." I toy with him and even reach up over my head to hang off his neck before he kisses me on the lips. My entire body stretches out, with bubbles failing to cover me.

"I think," he pulls away, "that we should head to bed, rest, or maybe I lay you down and relax you. You can't lift a finger." Ford kisses me once more then encourages me to scoot up so he can stand, and the sound of water moving fills the room.

Ford grabs a towel to wrap around his taut waist and

heads into the other room. I step out of the tub, grab the terrycloth robe, wrap it around my body, and then my world alters.

A pain as sharp as the day I labored Connor hits me. Gripping the sink mantel for support is useless because I fall to the floor, and my world goes dark.

FORD

I hold Brielle's hand as she lies in the hospital bed, with the sound of monitors beeping in the background. Her eyes slowly begin to flutter open, and I'm quick to swirl my fingers along the back of her hand.

The nurse who was reading her screen gives me a nod.

I've been sitting here for what feels like hours, worried and terrified. I'm not even going to comment on how I must look like shit because it's nothing compared to her ordeal.

"Elle, baby, hey," I attempt to greet her back into the world again. She woke a few times already, but she was out of it, so I bet she doesn't remember.

"Ford." Her voice is dry and groggy. She blinks a few times, and I can tell she is trying to register where she is.

"You're okay."

"Where am I again?" She attempts to move but winces in the process.

The nurse touches her arms to encourage her not to move. "Sweetie, you're in the hospital. I'm going to grab the doctor, okay?" The nurse leaves the room.

"Hospital, oh yeah," Brielle seems confused, as she

should be. "Fuck, why does it feel like I just gave birth or something?"

My lips twitch before I bring her hand to my mouth for a kiss. "You gave birth to your appendix, if that counts?" I do my best to keep this situation light.

She groans at the realization. "That's what was happening?"

"Yeah, I'm afraid so. You had emergency surgery."

"I recall something vaguely." She seems to be taking in her surroundings. "Where's Connor?"

"Still with my sister, he knows you're here. Violet will bring him later."

The doctor and the nurse returning to the room bring a sense of reality.

The woman in her fifties with glasses gives us a polite smile. "Brielle, you're awake again. I'm Dr. Thorpe." She comes to stand near Brielle's monitor. "You gave everyone quite a scare, but the good news is appendicitis is quite a common occurrence, and now with your appendix gone, you never have to worry about getting it out again."

"How did this happen?" Brielle asks, a bit weary.

"There are many reasons why this can occur, stress and digestion to name a couple. Luckily, your fiancé called an ambulance and got you here in time so we could do a laparoscopic surgery before the appendix ruptured. That means a quicker recovery time too. Within five days you should probably feel like nothing happened. We gave you antibiotics as a preventive matter because you can be more prone to infection now."

Brielle attempts to move again but whimpers from the pain, which in turn causes me to tense. I fucking hate seeing her this way and wish I could somehow make it better.

The doctor places her hand on Brielle's shoulder. "Rest. You can start to move around later today."

"I'll make sure she rests." I'm firm, and the doctor smiles at me.

"I'm confident you will have a full recovery," the doctor mentions again. "You can go home tomorrow; I want to monitor you for one more day."

"I can't even move." Brielle seems horrified.

The doctor laughs in a comforting way. "It feels like that, I'm sure, but I promise as soon as you start moving, it will quickly get better."

I notice Brielle's other hand touch her stomach, and she must feel the bandages.

"They say it is minimal scarring," I tell her.

The doctor nods. "The bandage is bigger than the wound. You have a small incision by your belly button and another one on your side; it will look like a mole."

"Oh." Brielle swallows, and I grab the bottle of water on the side table. She must be thirsty. "What does this mean if I ever want to…"

The doctor looks between us and registers the question. "Have a baby, I presume is what you're asking?"

"Yeah," Brielle shyly responds.

"You'll be fine. Some people find removing the appendix actually helps with fertility and others say to monitor for ectopic pregnancy, but in most cases, there are no problems. Speaking of which, we did take out your IUD as a precaution to prevent infections from spreading, so you will need to make an appointment with your gynecologist to get a new one."

"Sure. So, how long after recovery can we…"

My eyes grow impressed that my girl's mind is already there.

The doctor chortles a laugh. "Probably already in a week or two you can resume intercourse. Rest, and I will check on you during my next rounds." The doctor smiles one more time before mumbling something to the nurse about offering pain medication.

It doesn't take long for Brielle and me to be alone again.

"I was so fucking worried. Going out of my mind," I admit.

She squeezes my hand. "Now you know how I felt every time you had a hockey injury."

Hell. That's what I've put her through so many times. Even worse is I kept her as my emergency contact for most of the last ten years, so she couldn't escape it. Then again, I never had anything close to this. My injuries were mostly concussions and the occasional sprains.

"Well, you've paid me back in full. That was fucking scary. I don't ever want to think what life would be like without you in it."

Brielle looks at me strangely. "Now you're freaking me out. The doctor did just say that it was a standard procedure, right?"

"She did. Doesn't mean I didn't go out of my damn mind." I offer her the bottle of water that I forgot was in my hand. I bring the bottle to her lips, and she slowly takes a sip, then I set the drink to the side.

A laugh accompanied by a whimper comes from Brielle. "Wait a second... I don't remember so clearly, but wasn't I in a towel and nothing else?"

I grin to myself, more because I love how she is doing her best to be in positive spirits. "I found you on the bathroom floor, and yes, you had a robe on, nothing else. I was so concerned and in shock that I didn't even think to at least get more coverage, so some paramedic got an eyeful."

"Hope he was hot." She's taunting me.

"You must be feeling better if you can throw that line at me, knowing damn well it makes me insane."

She moves her head against the pillow, looking at me from a different angle. She still looks weak but nothing like last night when we brought her in. I don't even think she realizes that she was in and out of consciousness for a good part of the night; they gave her a lot of painkillers.

"I'm trying to forget that the last few days have been a complete disaster."

My heart aches again. This is a time when she should be celebrating. She has worked so hard, and if I'm honest, made the most sacrifices. This isn't fair in the slightest.

"I'm sorry, Elle."

I can faintly make out that she shrugs a shoulder. "Not your fault."

"Still."

"Fiancé, huh?" She attempts to keep her face neutral, but I see the line of her mouth twitch.

I lean back in my chair, a little bit proud, not of my move but for the fact that, for a little bit anyways, I got to play the part of her future husband again. "You're more than my girlfriend, and it was the easiest explanation."

"You really are getting bold."

"Only when it comes to you." She smiles lazily before she yawns. "Get some rest. I'll go grab you some real food, and I think you deserve some fresh flowers or a teddy bear from the gift shop."

She nods once before her eyes close again. I watch her for a few moments, taking in the view of my sleeping angel before I leave her room.

———

AFTER STOCKING up on food supplies and a few gifts from the hospital shop, I make my way back to Brielle's floor.

Alone in the elevator, I reflect that the last time I saw Brielle in the hospital as a patient was when our son was born.

I wasn't there at the start. I had to drive down from a game that I was supposed to have. Brielle's mom was with her, and although her mother was kind enough to acknowledge that it was a special moment for us, she only let Brielle and I have a few minutes together. Brielle was in pain then, but I dare say nothing compared to last night, which is why I felt like the earth was shattering.

When the doors of the elevator open, I walk out and turn the corner. I feel like I'm stepping out into déjà vu because there by Brielle's door are her parents, and for some godforsaken reason, my own father.

My body instantly tenses, and my face hardens. Why they are all here is a surprise, or maybe it shouldn't be. I called Brielle's parents when she was in surgery because it's the decent thing to do. It's what I would want if Connor was ever in a similar situation, but having everyone here is kind of the last thing Brielle needs.

Throughout the years, we've all kept our distance from one another. Respecting everyone's roles, yet in no way becoming a tight family unit. As much as I hate to admit it, even shitty parents can become amazing grandparents, and that's what they all are to Connor. The only time that we really all come face to face is Connor's birthday once a year or the occasional hockey game that Connor may play.

But here we are now, and I can't read anyone's expression.

Brielle's parents, Kerry and Jim, are the first to step forward. Her mom is soft in features, and her temperament is much like Brielle's, which means she is the least of my concerns.

"We were worried," Kerry mentions.

It's understandable. "I can imagine. Sorry, I was going to call again when Brielle is settled. Have you seen her?"

"Not yet." She holds onto her husband's arm.

"Strange timing, huh?" Jim's face is solidified, and accompanied by his dark polo and peppered hair, then he isn't exactly the picture of peace.

I set the bag of food on a chair nearby. "What does that mean?"

"Jim," Kerry nearly scolds him.

He shakes off Kerry's hold. "No. Just when Brielle finally gets everything she's waited for, he has to come right in and screw it up for her again."

"What the hell? How is appendicitis my fault?" I'm quick to defend.

"Stress. Commotion. You couldn't wait to throw a relationship at her until after the biggest exam of her life? The nurse let it slip that you two are engaged!" Jim is clearly pissed off at me.

My hands form fists at my sides, and I do my best to stay calm. I shake my head, choosing to ignore him, and instead my eyes catch my father giving Jim a stern eye.

"Why are you here?" I ask.

My father, with his blue eyes and near-black hair, quickly responds, "Violet explained the situation, and I was in the city for a meeting. They just went to the vending machine."

"Probably to escape you all," I mutter to myself. Scratching my cheek, I know I need to go into action mode. "Listen, Brielle needs rest. I'm not sure it's a good idea that everyone is here. She probably wants to see Connor and then focus on getting out of here."

"She must be devasted that she didn't get to give her best shot at the Bar exam," her father points out.

I glance to him, internally agitated. "Of course she is. But we can't change what happened, since appendicitis can happen at any moment due to biology," I grit out. "We can't go back in time."

He scoffs a sound. "Oh, that we know."

"Let it go," my father suggests.

I hold my hand to stop him because I'm capable of doing this on my own. "Go on, Jim, clearly you have a strong opinion on something."

"I do. It's so easy for you to stand there and bring our daughter flowers because everything you wanted career-wise you got, and now with your checklist of career goals all completed, the one moment Brielle may also get that chance, then you selfishly become a distraction, and now look where we all are." Her dad is seething.

He pushes that sore point inside of me. I hate what he is saying because I believe almost all of it. Maybe he is fucking right.

But I won't let him have the upper hand.

I step forward, puffing out my shoulders. "No. We wouldn't be in this position at all if you just let us stay together. We followed your lead because we were young and confused. But the tables have turned, and we don't need any of your support for anything, and I don't have to stand here and listen to why you think I'm still hell-bent on ruining Brielle's life when it's the opposite."

"You should have waited to throw all your intentions at her," he informs me with his voice raised.

I scoff a sound as I slide the back of my finger along my upper lip. "She already knew my intentions; we just never said it out loud." Inside I'm raging. "You know what, *Jim*?

Today is about Brielle, but make no mistake that we were both miserable. I gave up the woman and family that I wanted to ensure they both had a good life. Do you have any clue what that does to a man?"

"I think we all need to take a breather," my father recommends.

I side-eye him. "Why are you here? Like really, why are you here? Want to join Jim on the 'I fucked up in some way' train? Or are you here because you want to take the opportunity to point out some ridiculous flaw when Brielle is weak?"

He attempts to place his hand on my shoulder, but I shrug it off. "I'm on your team, I swear."

"A little late. Could have used that ten years ago when you pointed out Brielle was going to ruin my career because we were keeping Connor."

A twinge of pain flashes on my father's face. For a second, I might even think it's regret.

The sound of the door cracking open draws all our attention to Brielle who is standing in her hospital gown holding onto her IV stand, with the nurse behind her. She uses the door for support.

"What's going on out here?" She looks near baffled when she realizes who is in attendance at this gathering.

I step to her, wanting to pretend all is swell, and focus on helping her. "Everyone is just concerned. Look at you, already walking." I attempt to stretch a smile.

"The nurse here." She indicates with her head behind her. "She's a little strict and made me try walking. The yelling was just a coincidental incentive to move." Brielle sounds less than enthused.

"Yeah," I draw it out. "We were just having a *discussion*."

"Liar," she mumbles to me before she attempts to smile at her mom.

Her mom who, like always, stays out of the drama, reaches to touch Brielle's arm. "We're so happy it's just your appendix. You'll be on the mend real quick."

"Why did I hear you all talking about Connor?" Brielle asks.

Crap, she heard, and that means we triggered her mama bear button.

"It doesn't matter." I know that's not true, but I can at least try.

"How about you all move into Brielle's room not to disturb the other patients," the nurse orders more than she suggests.

We all look at one another and seem to agree without words to step into Brielle's room. It takes a minute for her to get settled on her bed again, but already she looks better than even an hour ago. Though, her face has lost any ounce of positive momentum we had when she woke. My eyes circle the room, and I get it. Our parents are here with serious looks and arms crossed.

When the nurse leaves, Brielle opens her mouth immediately. "I guess we are going to do this now?"

Her father pipes up, no surprise. "We're happy you're okay now, sorry this happened."

"But…" Brielle waits.

"It doesn't matter. I was just chatting with your *fiancé* man to man."

I swipe a hand across my jawline. "Something like that."

"We were going to talk to you all soon about our new relationship status, whatever you want to call it." Brielle avoids anyone's eye contact, and I internally feel victorious that she didn't correct her father about the fiancé title. "It can't be surprising."

"Maybe sudden," my father points out.

I shake my head. "You've all watched us punish ourselves for years."

To my surprise, Kerry speaks. "You both needed to find your way back to each other in your own time."

"*After* our daughter got everything she wanted," her father adds.

Brielle throws her arms up, and I can tell she felt something pull. "Yeah, I know, I failed the Bar, so let's add on another eight months to the '*will I ever accomplish what I was supposed to*' speech."

I want to scream at her not to let them get to her, but maybe now the post-surgery adrenaline is wearing off and she recognizes that her father might have a point.

"We can't go in a circle about this," my father volleys.

I blow out a breath, already exhausted from this.

"Easy for you to say, your son got everything. Brielle just sacrifices over and over for Ford and Connor." Her father clearly hates me, that I've long thought but now established.

"You don't think I fucking know that?" I raise my voice. I'm the one who could probably define selfishness in the dictionary.

"What the hell, everyone," my sister loudly whispers and peeks around the corner of the door. "Knock it off, Connor will be here any second, and this is *not* what he can walk into."

We all nod, agreeing on something.

"Can you all go," Brielle requests, and she looks defeated.

It's when I look at her, study her, that I see it. A sadness in her eyes, and in this moment, I hope her father didn't get to her, because I know he was only highlighting the obvious.

And if I were her, then I would probably be the last person she wants to see.

She reaches for my hand. "Can I have a moment alone with Connor?"

Something inside of me sinks, it's near my heart.

Simply responding with a nod, I swallow my pride and fear that she's pushing me away.

19

BRIELLE

It's been a few days since I left the hospital. I decided to take Ford up on his offer to stay at his place. With school starting soon, he and Connor can spend time together, not to mention recovery while looking out at Lake Spark seemed idyllic.

For the most part, the pain has worn off. However, the feeling of general mourning and numbness doesn't fade for a near finish that wasn't mine. Resting against the lounge chair, I watch Connor and Ford throw a ball around in the swimming pool. I adjust my sunhat and do my best to enjoy the scene. No bikini today, instead one of Ford's old pairs of shorts and a tank top because it's easier on my bandages.

"Do you want something from inside?" my son asks me tentatively as he uses his strength to pull himself out of the pool.

"It's okay. I'm still on the last water you brought me." I smile weakly.

Ford's been taking care of me, our son dotes on me, and together they are determined to give me the most relaxing recovery period possible. They are a dream team.

Which is why I can't figure out why I'm so down. Well, I know why. I just can't form my thoughts clearly.

Ford walks up the pool steps, and it catches my breath. How could it not? Droplets of water run down his muscles, and when he grabs his towel to dry off, I'm given a complete show. The kind that women pay a lot of money for, and they have when he participated in charity auctions or appeared in some magazine spread. Now he's mine.

He sits down on the chair next to me. "How's the patient?"

"Not complaining about the view, that's for sure."

A proud smirk forms a line on his mouth. "Happy to oblige, but I haven't seen you smile much today."

"Still coming down from the explosion in my life—failing the Bar, appendicitis, and our parents treating us like we're teenagers again. Ford, if I wasn't on antibiotics then I would be insisting on a strong cocktail right now," I inform him.

His eyes lower to my own. "It will be okay. You'll get back up like you always do."

I don't want to be annoyed with Ford, but it's easy for him to say. He has trophies and millions already. I'm not the type to be jealous, but it's a lot easier said when you're in his shoes. I hate that my father's words seeped into my thoughts and won't escape; it's a pesky fly.

"Other than my text check-in with my mom, I haven't spoken to my dad since. You?"

He thins his lips. "No, haven't heard from my dad, but that's not exactly new."

I look over his shoulder to see that Connor is still busy in the kitchen. "He has no clue we're not thrilled with his grandparents, right?"

"Nah, remember they're all good at grandparenting.

Connor is only worried about you. He asked me this morning if you really lost your monkey tail, because apparently, the internet is telling him that's what appendices are."

I snort a laugh. "Cute." I hold the back of my sunhat as I feel a breeze. "We will miss being here."

Ford's eyes lock on me, and he cocks his head gently to the side. "You know how to solve that."

I lick my lips, giving myself a moment. "Connor has school, and we agreed he should finish there before he is off to middle school next year."

"I know, and Hollows is 45 minutes away provided there are no run-ins with foxes, ducks, or lost tourists. Just letting you know that if you want, this is all yours when the time comes."

I play with the drawstring of the shorts I'm wearing. "I guess I won't be a lawyer, so my job doesn't really factor into this anymore."

Ford reaches out to gently touch my shoulder. "You'll take the test again in February, it's not over."

I go wide-eyed, as if he's crazy. "Easy for you to say," I nearly bite it out.

A shade of hurt hits his demeanor because I know I've been pushing him away a little while I wallow in my disappointment.

The sound of the sliding door breaks our odd tension.

Our son wobbles as he carries a giant basket filled with food with a purple bow on top. "I think the neighbors left this."

Ford leaps out of his chair to quickly help Connor by taking the basket, and his head dips while he tries to read the card. "'Get well soon so we can ditch the guys and go for a spa day at the Dizzy Duck. Hugs, Piper and April.'"

I smile softly, as that was very sweet of them. I should

have made more of an effort to see them while I've been in Lake Spark, but life has been busy.

"Yes! We got April's coconut brownies." Connor is already exploring the care package.

"Back off, those are totally mine," I challenge.

Ford sets the basket down at the bottom of my recliner, and I sneak a peek at the array of snack options.

"Everyone was worried," Ford adds.

I sigh. "I know. I'm just a little lost about what to do next."

"Grandpa says you're going to come to your senses. I don't know what that means," Connor informs us as he chomps on a cookie.

Ford glances at me with a hardened smile, clearly unimpressed with my father's choice of words, and I can only rub my forehead, feeling Ford's sentiment.

"Your grandfather just needs some time to adjust to your father and me changing our relationship," I attempt to explain.

"We're not inviting him to Thanksgiving, huh?" Connor speaks in a sarcastic tone.

It causes me to half-smile and Ford to crack a grin.

For a second, I'm reminded of how happy I was before the explosion of my life.

———

THE THING about having a ten-year-old is once the sneaking around stopped, Ford and I were free to share a room with no fear of Connor interrupting us, as he is past that stage of childhood. It means Ford and I can get lost between the sheets, although on the quiet side.

I slide into bed with Ford who is already lying with the

duvet draped around his waist to reveal his shirtless body. His smirk informs me that he approves of my night dress that is cotton, simple yet short, and the straps fall off easily. I'm quick to find myself in his arms with my head resting against his chest.

"I'm worried," he states, meaning about me. He begins to draw lazy circles on the curve of my shoulder.

"I know." I focus on trailing my fingers on the outline of his pecs. "I'm just so disheartened. I know it's just an exam but passing it would be the trophy that confirms I did it all despite getting pregnant at eighteen."

He places a soft kiss on the top of my head, but he doesn't say anything.

"You're lucky, Ford."

I feel him tense slightly. He feels guilty, and I'd be lying if I said a slither of resentment didn't flow through me.

"I'm only lucky because of you." His voice is delicate. "Is it just the exam bothering you? Or is it our parents?"

"I don't like remembering the way it was, and now here we are ten years later, and our parents still manage to make me feel like we are incapable of making decisions for ourselves. It was shitty, that's for sure." And sad and infuriating. I'm twenty-eight, and they make me feel like a child.

"We either confront them or move on. When we were younger, they put pressure on us, but they don't have that power over us anymore. They have no choice but to accept us or let it all go."

A disgusted sound escapes me. "Until they decide they need to speak their mind."

Ford is careful when he slides out from under me to lie on his side against a propped arm. "That's on me. I'm the one telling everyone you're my fiancée, and deep down I wanted them to find out, not from us. How fucked up is that?"

I reach up to cradle his face. "It's called bitterness, and we are allowed to feel it. Ten years, Ford. Ten years that we could've had it all."

"And now when we have the chance for everything, and you miss your opportunity to have something for yourself," he subtly notes.

My head bows. "I'm used to it."

He kisses the palm of my hand that rests on his face. "You'll get everything. I'll wait with you until you do. If I had a way to fix this, you have to know I would."

I nod before he places a kiss on my inner wrist, delicate and sweet.

"You never gave me the gift." He said he had one when we were at the hotel. "I guess I'm not entitled to it anymore."

He lowers his head and peers up at me. "Well, that's just a lie. You can have it. I just thought you might want the clouds to clear first."

"Show me."

Ford kisses my cheek before leaning across the bed to his side drawer, and he pulls out the box he had that day on the boat.

"I upgraded it a bit." He studies the black box before handing it to me.

"There was nothing to upgrade." I open the box, and I can't help but smile. The diamond looks a little bigger.

"Look inside," he urges.

I squint my eyes an I study the inner band. "Worth the wait. F.B.C."

Our family initials and the words that will forever float around us.

"It's perfect. Let's get married. Tomorrow." I string together the sentence that is delicate, yet my certainty is there.

Ford laughs, and his head falls back on the pillow.

"Why is that funny? I'm serious," I protest.

He's on his side again, staring at me with a smirk. "Nothing would make me happier, but baby, you had an eventful week. I won't let you do something while you are in shock and not feeling yourself. You have a lot of emotions right now."

"Ford—"

He shushes my mouth with his finger. "Know it's there. Dream of our day. And I'm ready to confirm our future when you actually don't have a bandage on."

Maybe he has a point. My thoughts are everywhere. Closing the box with the ring inside, I set it to the side.

His thumb smudges my bottom lip. "How about some sleep?"

A sweet Ford who has a wicked look while he is shirtless is like a tornado forming. You're unsure of the strength, but either way, it's dangerous.

"I want you to make me feel good," I request. Sinking into the mattress and melting into his touch is my escape, the best pain reliever.

"Not a good idea. You're still recovering."

I clasp his fingers near my mouth and guide them down to the fabric of my night dress around my breast. "I'm fine, and I *need* you."

His face informs me that he is conflicted because he doesn't want to hurt me, but he wants me. Always a perfect combination for passion.

Ford's jaw flexes to the side; he's contemplating.

Please, I mouth.

"Lie down, head on the pillow."

I adjust myself, breathing out as I get comfortable.

"You're not going to move a damn inch," he orders before he swivels down the bed.

"What are you up to?" I raise a brow.

He doesn't bother replying with words. Instead, he spreads my thighs, groaning when he finds my pussy bare. It's not a surprise, I never sleep with panties.

His eyes are filled with hunger, and his lips dragging up my skin just hits different this time. Everything inside of me is heightened, sensitive, and aching, but one look at him and it's a confirmation that it's the good kind of pain. It's yearning.

He spreads my lips open, sliding a finger along my center, then softly growls as he lowers his mouth to me. I gasp from his wet tongue hitting my clit, especially when he laps up my juices, and I recognize that he is starving for me. It's been days since we've been intimate like this.

My eyelids become heavy as endorphins take over my body. Thankfully, Ford holds me down for stability, keeping my thighs parted.

"I could lick you all night," he whispers, then his tongue circles.

A wave begins to form inside my body. My fingers dig into his hair to usher him away. "More of you." My breath is beginning to run ragged.

His finger dips inside of me, and I clench around him. This isn't enough. I want it all.

I'm allowed to be greedy right now. Everyone is allowed to have a down period and someone who can help them through it.

Ford moans when he inserts another finger. His teeth grab hold of my dress, and he slowly drags it up, pausing when he sees the bandage on my belly.

"I'm fine," I promise. "But I want you inside of me." I breathe, my body arching as his fingers play with me.

"Elle—"

I grab hold of his wrist, drawing his fingers out of me, and I bring them to my lips for a taste. I need his attention, and I make it clear that recovery be damned, I want him inside of me. I suck, making a point for him to watch my mouth take every last drop.

"Please, you make me feel better," I beg again.

He kisses me, delving his tongue between my lips to open my mouth, stroking my tongue with his own, and making me dizzy in the process.

"Let me take you from behind," he whispers.

We get into a spooning position after he plops an extra pillow in front of me for my body to prop against while he wraps his arm around me. When he works his cock inside me, I feel like I can finally breathe in relief.

"We need to be careful." He kisses my shoulder as he begins to find his speed.

"I'm not in pain."

Our fingers link. "I meant you're not on birth control."

Oh yeah, that.

What a turn of events that at the start of the summer Ford was the one not using logic, and here I am now at the mercy of finding relief.

"Then pull out, just don't end this."

Something about my words causes him to spear into me, still careful yet more robust.

"Shh, just let go." He grazes my shoulder with his teeth. "We'll go slow, as long as it takes, but I'm going gentle."

Glancing behind my shoulder, I'm faced with his deter-mined eyes that are set on me. He made his claim on me long ago, and he takes his job to make me happy very seriously, which is why I feel him circling my clit with his finger again as he pumps in and out of me.

"I love you," I say and kiss him. My words seem to send him into his own world as he holds my hip down and dives deeper inside of me.

"We have our whole lives for me to enjoy you like this, but why does it feel like I need to reassure you?" he manages to ask just as I feel him hit that perfect spot between my internal walls.

"I'm not perfect. I'm lost," I admit.

"You're not lost. You just need to remember what you value the most."

I don't have time to answer because his mouth covers mine to capture my moan as I begin to shake around him, not even from an orgasm, he just works my body in the right ways.

His words don't leave me, though. I just need some time to breathe and figure out my thoughts that are all over the place.

Because we can't survive our hearts breaking twice.

20

FORD

As the days go by, Brielle seems to ease more. Well, at least I catch her smiling while she flips pancakes this morning, barefoot in my kitchen.

I head straight for my prize, wrap my arms around her middle, and sway us side to side. "You're spoiling him."

"It's pancakes." She laughs.

"You cook him full breakfasts every morning. Don't even try to hide it, I see your magic witchcraft."

"They're chocolate chips."

"Exactly."

Glancing over her shoulder, she flashes me an odd look. I just shut it down with a kiss.

She shimmies me away and stacks a plate with pancakes. "Come on, Connor will be down in a minute or two. I set the table outside."

"Okay, I'll grab my coffee." I walk to the machine and make my cup while she grabs a few items.

We walk together, and I take a plate from her so she doesn't need to juggle everything. I'm studying the bowl of scrambled eggs and questioning if Connor realizes he is treated like a prince when I nearly run into Brielle.

"No way!" Brielle shrieks and stops in her tracks when we open the sliding door.

I bump into her slightly before I realize she is frozen, and when I look forward, then I know why.

"Is that…" I angle my head to the side to study the pool.

"A raccoon."

We both stay in place because we don't want to scare away the raccoon that is literally swimming in the pool. It's like a little dog, paddling around in laps.

"This is not normal," she says, adamant.

"Just great, now I'm going to have to empty the pool," I whisper, not thrilled.

"Why?"

"He probably has rabies or something. Doesn't even seem fazed by us."

"I think he's just warm." Brielle takes a cautious step forward. "What do we do? Scare him away? Damn, if only we had a dog now."

I hand her the bowl of eggs I was carrying and take matters into my own hands. I pull out my phone, pull up a song, and turn the outside speakers on because clearly this animal finds us too quiet.

With the song now playing, Brielle looks at me and bursts out laughing.

The racoon finally notices that he has an audience and is quick to swim to the steps.

"Are you seriously scaring him away with Taylor Swift?" She's in hysterics now.

I shrug a shoulder. "You're messing with my playlist algorithm."

Her eyes study me. "Or you are just secretly a Swifty fan."

With the racoon running into the woods, Brielle stumbles her way to the table because she is ridiculously happy in this very moment.

I love that.

Joining her at the table, I bring her to my arms because the rumble of her laughter against my skin is therapy.

"Seriously, what the hell was that, right? I mean, it's never happened," I note.

She places her hand on my shoulder. "It's okay. Most guys are into Taylor Swift, you can admit it now. It's cool to like her."

I roll my eyes. "Not that. The raccoon."

"Oh, that. Yeah, I'm positive it's an omen."

"I'm going to be researching this all morning now."

Her laughter subsides, but it's still there.

"Dad, your tablet in the kitchen is going off. It's the front-gate app," Connor calls out from the door.

I wave to him in thanks then check the app on my phone. I see that we have a visitor at the security gate, as the app sends a notification.

I curse under my breath when I see who is on the other side. I show Brielle the screen.

And there goes any morsel of happiness on Brielle's face.

She straightens her posture. "Why is my father here?"

"I don't know." I turn to Connor. "How about you take your pancakes and go watch some TV or read your book."

Connor doesn't protest.

Checking with Brielle, I know our great morning now took a sharp turn. We were not expecting Brielle's dad, that's for sure.

We both give one another a look of recognition and confirmation.

We'll face him.

And a few minutes later, we do just that.

Brielle's father appears from around the corner of the house, since I told him we were out back.

"Was the raccoon an omen for this?" I mumble as Brielle leans into my arm.

Her father slows in his approach, pausing at a distance from us. "I guessed you would be here."

"You could have called and asked if you really wanted to find me," she mentions.

"It's okay, it's just the proof that you haven't been thinking clearly the last few weeks."

I stand tall and my shoulders roll back. "What the hell does that mean?"

"She's so blinded by your charm that she fails to see she is always following your lead." Jim is coming out swinging, clearly.

Brielle waves her hands in the air between us, doing her best to break the tension. "I'm right here, you know. I think I can speak for myself."

Her father turns his attention to her. "You're really going to marry him?"

"Why would it be a bad thing? Whatever you may think, even if you choose to ignore the fact that I love him, Ford is Connor's father, he will always be in our lives."

"Can't you see it? Everything is always on his damn timeline. Every decision has been around him, and you fool yourself by saying every decision is for Connor."

I step forward, ready to defend, because if I believed in fighting then I would strangle him right about now, and the same thought keeps circling back to me, as it has been the last few weeks. I can't decide if it's because he is planting theories in her head or if it's because I believe it.

"What's the point of coming here? We already heard you back at the hospital," I inform him.

"I'm concerned for my daughter. She's been through a lot lately, and your rushed reunion is cause for care."

Brielle sneers and brings her hands to her hips. "Lately? I've been through a lot *lately*? Why don't we rewind to when you told us that you would only support me if we agreed that Ford and I couldn't be together."

"It was for the best. The statistics on young parents staying together are slim."

I swipe my hands through my hair as I blow out a tight breath. "If you care to disrespect us, then please get off my damn property."

"Exactly, *your* property. You dangle a reunion in front of my daughter, after you build a house that she had no say in, in a place where maybe she doesn't even want to live. You set the parameters for all of her decisions going forward."

"What? As opposed to you and the first years of Connor's life? I'd sell it all if she wants, but look around, and then maybe you'll see that I've only ever had her on my mind. This is her house because I built it with her in my thoughts, down to the bench swing that I know she loves."

Jim searches Brielle's face, but he struggles as she lowered her head. "I'm your father. I'll give you advice whether you want it or not, and I'm going to say that I think you need to slow down because you or Connor don't want to get hurt if you realize that the relationship you had in your head isn't what you dreamed about when you were eighteen."

"You need to go," I snipe.

Brielle has gone quiet, and I can tell she wants to burst into tears.

"Is that what you want, sweetie?" he has the audacity to ask her.

"I think it's for the best," she sniffles.

I grab his arm to lead him away, but he yanks it back, ignoring me. "I do love you, Brielle. Remember, your mother and I supported you and Connor, always have and will."

"You may have been there at the start when we were confused," I snap. "The moment I could, I provided for her. Through the years, you and I, we've managed to be respectful. Thanks for ruining that streak," I say, sarcastic.

"We all know that we will do anything for Connor. Make no mistake, Ford, the moment you moved in on Brielle again, I was reminded of what you will always be."

"And what's that?"

"You'll always be the guy who got my barely eighteen-year-old pregnant who then put her life on hold while you got your hockey dreams."

"Enough!" Brielle holds her palm up, and she's now over the edge of calm. "Get out, please," she begs.

A stiff moment of silence overcomes us before Jim gets a clue and nods goodbye to his daughter.

He disappears around the house, and I turn to look at Brielle who has a red face, tears streaming.

Instantly, I pull her into a hug with her face buried into my chest. "I'm so sorry."

She sobs for a good minute or two, until the moment she pulls away and peers up to me. "I don't know what is worse right now. Everyone looking at me with pity or feeling like I should check that I'm not blinded by lust and missing a clue."

"No. Do *not* do that. Don't let him get to you," I urge with extreme worry and fear.

She doesn't answer.

We've had distance between us before, but it's a thousand times worse when I'm literally holding her in my arms. She's the person who made me believe that all the hope we've both carried was for a reason, because us together could finally be within our grasp.

21

FORD

Sitting at a table in Catch 22, I pass a small toy to Hudson's and Piper's daughter. Hudson is busy cutting up pieces of chicken on a plate. He has a daddy afternoon that he managed to fit into his schedule, and we agreed to meet for lunch. It's a cloudy day, as the last days of summer are here.

"You okay with Connor back at school and Brielle in Hollows?" he asks as he slides the plate to Gracie who attempts to pick up a few pieces with her fingers.

"I mean, I would rather they be here, but it's doable. I try to head there once during the week, and they come here on the weekends. Maybe the space is also a good thing." I'm not going to lie, I've felt a little down lately.

Hudson gives me the once-over. "She's still not feeling great, huh?"

"Physically she's fine. I think she has come to terms with the Bar exam and the idea that she has to repeat the test, but it's more our parents being complete idiots that really triggered her."

"Did she even get her test results yet?"

"No, but she said that she blanked out on the last section, so it isn't possible to get the score she needs. Anyway, she isn't sure what to do career-wise. I also don't ask anymore. I recognize that there are maybe more opportunities in Chicago than there are here, and I'd be lying if I said that I didn't wish for certainty that she would end up here. I mean, I'll follow her wherever."

Hudson grabs his iced tea. "Give it time. When the results come in, then maybe more clarity will come."

I scoff a sound and grab a fry. "We have a few weeks still, but I already told Connor to check the mail so he can grab the envelope before Brielle sees it, then I can guarantee I'm there for her when she opens it."

"And your parents?"

Grabbing another fry, I smile bitterly to myself. "Her parents hate me. Or at least her dad. We had a big blowout the other week."

"Have you tried talking to him?"

"Hell no, I'm not going to waste my breath."

Hudson leans back and grins. "Don't do that. You're a man now who has maturity and class. Be the man you would want your own daughter to marry."

"I don't have a daughter," I rebuff.

"But I do, and I'm older and wiser. Trust me, you may never see eye to eye, but at least be able to say you tried."

I groan because he's right. I owe it to Connor and Brielle at least.

"I have my own father to deal with first. Besides, I feel guilty," I admit. "Her father may have a point. I threw a lot at Brielle this summer, for my own advantage."

Hudson checks on Gracie's eating progress before fixing his gaze on me. "Love makes us do crazy things. The last time I checked, the two of you aren't new. I also don't think entering into a relationship that's been years in the making needs a right date. Love is organic, so it works in its own time."

I tip my chin up. "I kind of pushed fate along on this one."

"And she didn't run away."

"I just…" I bite my inner cheek, frustrated. "I hate that her dad is so damn right. She sacrificed more."

"You can't change what was done. You both have to learn to let it go."

"I feel like I can only do that once I know she is at peace with how the cards fell. I feel like she is lost a little right now, and I hate that." I rub my temples with my fingers. I'm stressed to say the least.

Hudson curls a finger to rub his upper lip. "Patience can be the best medicine. I don't particularly have it, but I know that sometimes people need to figure out something on their own before they return to you."

"I wasn't sure if that's the philosophy that I should follow, but grand gestures and ultimatums don't seem fitting right now."

He taps the table with his knuckle. "Then wait."

I nod and turn my attention to Gracie who squeals and has ketchup all over her face, and it's hard not to smile weakly at that.

"By the way, my sister asked about Brielle." As she probably would since Brielle interned for her a while back. "She wants to meet up with her to give career advice but only after Brielle gets her Bar results, because she believes that you shouldn't plan on a maybe. Lawyers like hard facts."

"I appreciate that."

"She also mentioned that there is a small practice in the

county over that will have someone retiring in the spring. She could put in a good word."

I hold my hand up. "As much as I would love for Brielle to work in law and be permanently in Lake Spark, it needs to come from her. I'm not going to push it. I've done enough lately to play with fate."

He smiles to himself. "You'll look back at all of this one day and it will make sense, I promise."

I tap my finger in the air to show I hear him and quite frankly believe him too.

———

Sitting across from Margo, I admire how she always has fresh tea and cakes at the ready in her conservatory. Granted, my sister has already been here for an hour, so my last-minute visit is a coincidence for Margo's social etiquette. I only phoned her this morning.

Violet pours me some tea that I will never drink, but I can't say no in front of Margo. "After graduation, and as soon as I have enough money, I think I need to set my roots somewhere."

"Of course you do, dear. You're beautiful, and a man will want to snap you up. They are more inclined if you show stability." Margo places her teacup back on the saucer.

I have to chortle because I know Margo is only partly joking.

"Flowers. I'm good with flowers." Violet seems to ignore Margo's statement and speak to herself.

Margo turns her attention to me. "I've been waiting for you to come back to me."

I fold my arms over my chest and lean back. "Why is that?" I ask dryly.

"I'm not a fool, I know your engagement story with Brielle had a few holes. But I appreciated the effort and the fun I had phoning the flower shop. Your parents were shocked for sure when they found out at the hospital. I'm not sure why, though, it's a perfect love story that you both finally get your reunion." Margo seems to be reflecting.

Violet raises her brows at me.

Blowing out a long breath, I adjust my posture in the seat, leaning forward with my elbows on my thighs. "I might have embellished a few facts, but it was also the catalyst to, well… a lot."

"I gathered. I heard a few whispers from your sister when I asked where to send flowers to Brielle after the hospital." She looks up when I hear someone enter the room behind me. "There you are," she smiles proudly.

My eyes land on my father.

Violet leans to my side to whisper, "Truthfully, you've been kind of set up."

I roll my eyes.

"Ford." My father's greeting is short.

"Hello." I can't bring myself to look at him.

"How is Brielle?" He attempts to sound concerned.

Now it grabs my attention. "You care?"

"Of course, she is Connor's mother."

Violet taps her fingers on the table. "Look at you two talking," she says in an attempt to make peace.

"I think you two need to talk like men. Neither Violet nor I are in the mood for children at our table," Margo informs us without losing a moment of dropping a sandwich on her plate.

"You planned this?" I ask Margo.

"You know me, breezing in like a southern wind when you need it." A proud smirk is hinted on her lips.

My eyes turn to my father who is staring at me, before my sister pulls on his arm so he sits down next to her.

Violet clears her throat, indicating for my father to speak.

"It's good we're here. Gives us a chance to talk. I didn't want to disturb you the past few weeks, as I know your focus has been on Brielle and her recovery."

"Yes, and?"

"At the hospital, it occurred to me that you might still hold a grudge against me for how things went down back then."

"That's an understatement." I don't even look at him.

My sister kicks me under the table, informing me that I should be more open to this conversation. Looking up, I see that my father hasn't lost his focus on me.

"I can't change the past, but I need to point out that I think you and Brielle together now makes sense."

My head perks up in surprise. "You what?" I need to double-check.

"You have my full support."

"Why now?" I'm wary.

"You're a real adult now, and Connor is older. You should get everything you worked for, including Brielle." An audible breath escapes him, and he seems surprised by his own admission.

My eyes search Margo and Violet, and they both give a reassuring smile.

"Didn't Briclle ruin my life, according to you?"

A sneer plays on his lips. "I did say something like that once, but the reality is that it takes two to create a pregnancy, plus people change, and Brielle has always been a sweet person."

Violet shakes her head at me. "Don't question the why, but he is genuine, we talked about it."

"I think you have enough on your plate, and I don't want you to think I'm an extra block," my father adds.

I rub my forehead with my hand before taking a deep breath, wondering if aliens landed somewhere.

"Sometimes reconciliation is easy and simple," Margo mumbles to me.

Everyone waits for me to say something, and I'm just struggling to digest the last few minutes.

Maybe they're right, sometimes we don't need to question more.

"I appreciate it," I manage to say. My eyes meet my father's. I'm still skeptical yet convinced enough. To be honest, other than the moment when I told him Brielle was pregnant, he's been supportive for almost everything.

Violet claps her hands together. "Hug it out. You know you want to."

Slightly awkward, but what the hell. Margo is right and we should take the wins without question sometimes.

Reluctantly, or rather unsure, I stand at the same time as my father, and we hug it out. In the awkward-as-fuck, half-a-hug kind of way. I'm not sure why some odd dose of chemicals hits me, but I'm slightly affected, not in a bad way.

"See? I needed this before I move. You get the girl, closure with your father, and a fuck-you to Jim. I hope you all visit me down in Florida." Margo drinks from her tea.

We all look to one another and have to smile.

———

LATER, when I'm back home and staring out my living room window with a glass of scotch hanging from my hand, I take the energy of the day and decide to extend an olive branch.

Phoning Brielle's father, I wait for him to pick up. The rim of the glass hits my lips for one last sip.

"Ford," her father greets me.

Blowing out a breath, I rip the band-aid off. "Listen, we both want what is best for Brielle. You have your theories about me, and I'm only going to tell you that you're right. I'm a selfish asshole. But the thing is, I don't care. If it means I get Brielle and can make her happy every day, then fine, call me selfish. I've waited ten fucking years for your daughter. There isn't anything that I wouldn't do for her. You either accept it or move on, because here is another thing, Jim. She's going to be my wife, and I have no problem flaunting that fact in front of you for the years to come, because Brielle and I make one another happy. You don't need to watch out for her, I'm her protector now. Whether you can move on or not, just know that she's in good hands, and ten years can make your love for someone become unbreakable."

Hitting the red button, I toss my phone to the sofa and finish my drink.

Not exactly an olive branch, but that felt damn good.

BRIELLE

I hand my glass to Lena so she can give me a refill. We're sitting on my sofa discussing life while enjoying wine and snacks.

"I'll miss you if you move to Lake Spark," she tells me for the millionth time.

"It's not the other side of the earth. Besides, I'm not really sure we can make Lake Spark work because of wherever my career heads." I swirl the wine around inside my glass.

"Huh." She seems to be considering my words.

I take a sip of the wine. "What?"

"I know we're mothers, so we tend to put our kids first, and you are allowed to have something for yourself, but the lawyer thing…" My eyes flutter while I wait for her to finish her sentence. "Is it actually what you want? Or is it what you think you want?"

"Of course it's what I want," I protest.

"I'm merely pointing out that sometimes we are so set on an idea that we want to see it through, even when we may have fallen out of love with it. I mean law, not Ford."

Setting my wine glass on the coffee table, I understand

where Lena is coming from. "It was a lot of years of studying to just let it all go. I want to see it through. Does it matter if I change paths later? At least it would be on my own terms."

Lena grabs the chocolate. "The lawyer title would be your trophy to show everyone you achieved what you set out to do."

I roll a shoulder to the side. "Maybe. But I also really do want to succeed at it."

"I think Ford may be the reward. You get to enjoy rewards, trophies you just stare at." She smirks.

"That's a solid point. Anyway, I'm happy school has started again, and we can find a routine. This summer was a whirlwind." I exhale loudly.

"Yet despite your hospital visit and crazy parents, you still have a smile that doesn't seem to leave you. That's a great sign."

"It is, isn't it? Wish my mind would catch up," I admit.

"Sometimes I wonder if we really can have it all. If we always need to sacrifice something, you know, juggling motherhood, career, romance. It is possible, as long as you know that if someone were to snap their fingers, you close your eyes, and the first thing that comes to you is what is important. You know that you probably won't see it all, but one thing. Tell me, the last few years, if you closed your eyes, what did you see?"

That's easy, and instantly a soft smile graces my lips. "Ford and Connor."

She splays her hands out to the side. "Voila, you have both of them. Life is pretty amazing right now. You just need to focus on that."

I laugh. "Trust me, I would love to forget that Ford and my father are completely on the outs."

"Does it get to you what your dad said? Do you believe you follow Ford's lead?"

My lips roll in then quirk out as I twist the stem of the wine glass between my fingers. "Doesn't someone always lead in a relationship?"

This time I catch Lena out, as she seems to be contemplating my words. "That normally means someone is waiting. Sounds like you both have been. Besides, Ford threw everything on the table and now he is giving you space and time. Isn't that what he's doing?"

I don't hesitate. "He is."

"Then tell your father to get a grip."

"I should," I admit. "Especially since I think everything is clearer to me. Life is filled with mixed moments. This summer has been amazing when it comes to Ford and me. Meh on the other stuff. But it's okay, the incredible stuff is what matters."

She taps my glass with her own. "Great. Then don't let anything else get you down, and if it does, then know it's most likely fixable."

It is.

———

MY MOTHER BUSIES herself in the kitchen of my childhood home while I sit across from my father in the living room. "I'll be quick. As long as you don't disrespect Ford in front of Connor, you can continue to see Connor. But if you can't support my relationship with Ford, then I think it's best we don't communicate for a while."

My father brings one knee over the other. "He's now come between us."

"You haven't given me much choice. Clearly, you can't see how happy he makes me."

"You've been miserable for years because of him," he points out.

I shake my head once. "I've been miserable because I thought we weren't possible. We are, and I'm not going to keep repeating how the last years have played out. I get my chance at absolute happiness, and I'm not letting it go."

"It may seem that way—"

"Stop." I hold my hand up. "You either support us or not. I won't go in circles. I'm not a girl confused and trying to figure out how to care for a baby. I'm a woman now who will stand up for anything that gets in the way of what will make my life good."

My father leans back and scratches his chin. "He phoned me, you know."

"Ford?"

"Made it clear that I should accept you two. No matter what I think, either way he intends to make you his bride one day and will enjoy flaunting that."

I attempt to smother a smile because that sounds like him. "As much as I love him for doing that, I'm here to tell you that you should accept everything because *I made* the decision that it's what I want."

He seems to be slightly calmer.

"It's kind of a pain in the ass having two men in my life so hot-headed," I add. If there was ever a chance for light-heartedness in this moment, then it's now.

"Ford and I are not the same," he interjects.

Okay, that was a failed attempt to find middle ground.

"We were all fine until Ford and I changed our status. All I'm asking is we get back on the same damn train." I'm now agitated that we're going in a circle.

"You seem miserable," he notes.

"There is plenty that has gone wrong this summer, but Ford Spears is not the reason. The best moments lately have been because of him."

"It's not just this summer."

I swallow, well aware that I'm not going to drag this afternoon on. "What if I told you I heard what you were saying? But I've made peace with how everything played out. I have a future ahead of me, and that's what I will focus on."

"Brielle." His tone is still too stern for me.

I stand up. "Reach out when you're ready, because I am," I add right before I storm out, frustrated yet knowing that I won't let this situation alter my life.

By the time I'm in the car, I managed to get several grumbles out. Now sitting in the car, I reflect on the last few minutes, and surprisingly, I feel… free.

I'm grateful to my parents for their help, but I'm not indebted. I can make my own decisions, like any woman who knows exactly what they want.

Which is why I grab my phone and call Ford.

He answers on the second ring. I don't even let him say anything.

"You know I researched it and apparently raccoons *are* an omen."

"And?" His voice is gruff, full of interest.

"I found it's the sign you should be more aware of what's around you or you should be adaptable. It feels like life right now. Anyway, I think those are good omens." My voice is slightly whimsical, I must admit.

I can hear Ford's breath. "Sounds like good omens to have."

"I believe so."

"Where are you?"

"Outside my dad's house."

I hear him wince. "Yikes."

"It's okay. He's very much looking forward to your chat about making me your future bride," I tease him.

"Elle, you know I like to make a claim." His voice sounds equally cunning and possessive.

"Don't worry, I don't think any conversation will be happening any time soon, and I'm okay with that."

We hold through a brief silence.

"Everything will be all right," he promises.

I tap my steering wheel. "I'm beginning to see that."

23

FORD

onnor leans over the side of the ice rink to reach into his bag. He keeps his feet covered in skates crossed at the ankles to avoid hitting anyone as he grabs an envelope from his sports bag before plopping back onto the ice.

It's Friday, which means we're spending the weekend in Lake Spark after Brielle or I pick Connor up from school. Brielle did it this week, as I had meetings today with sponsors.

He offers me the letter. "I did what you asked."

Glimpsing down at the envelope, I can see that he did. I gently hit his head with the thin envelope before holding it up. "Thanks. It might be a rough night for your mom. These are her results."

"Why didn't you want her to open them?"

"Because according to everyone, I'm selfish, and I don't want her to open it alone. I want to be there for her," I explain.

Connor wipes his face with his shirt. "I think that will make her happy. That you're there."

"Hope so." I scoff out a breath. "Thanks for keeping our secret." I indicate with the envelope, and he offers me a soft smile. "Go. You can have ten more minutes on the ice, then we'll grab a pizza and head home." I stuff the envelope in the back of my jeans.

He tips his head up. "Okay, Mom's back."

Connor skates off, and I turn to see Brielle walking down the steps with a filled water bottle.

"There you are," she says softly. "I was looking for you when we arrived, but the front desk said that you were stuck in a meeting."

I walk a few steps to meet her and quickly kiss her before following her to sit down in the stands. Immediately, her eyes search for Connor who is circling the ice. It's easy to notice that there is something on Brielle's mind.

"You okay?"

She glances to me then back to the ice. "The drive here was peaceful. Only had to slow down once because of a family of ducks crossing."

I look at her peculiarly, as I feel like this is the start of a bigger conversation. "What is it, Elle? You seem different."

She swallows and places her hand on my thigh. "So many times, I've sat in a similar spot as now. Either to watch you or watch our son. I can't stop thinking about what it would be like if things were different, our timeline, goals."

I gently tuck a strand of her hair behind her ear. "And?"

She turns her head, with her eyes set on me, and the corner of her mouth twitches. "I would miss it. I've been doing a lot of reflection—and wine drinking, but mostly reflection. During all these years, I've been wishing for a few things, but there was one thing I wanted the most."

"Which is?" I feel like my heart just sank to my belly.

Have I gotten it all wrong? The last month or so, have I

been losing her? Is it possible that someone can slip through your fingers twice?

But then a reassuring smirk appears on her lips. "It's you. You, me, and Connor."

Relief hits me, and I take her hand between my palms because I feel she has more to say.

"I get to have that now, and it's enough."

I tip my head to the side. "I love that you say that, but I won't ever let you settle for less. I don't want you to feel like you're settling."

Her hand comes to my jawline, and she plays with the stubble on my chin with her thumb. "You don't seem to get it. I'll try again with the Bar and see what I do career-wise. It's just that you and Connor are by far more important, and I want to grab everything that I've been waiting for. I want to get married, I don't want to wait. We'll have an odd living situation for a bit, but at the end of the school year, Connor and I will move here."

I would protest if I thought she wasn't thinking from a clear place, but her voice and look say it all. She has thought it over, and she's serious.

Letting go of her hand, my fingers move to the back of her neck to pull her into a kiss. Our foreheads touch, and I make a point to keep us close. "If it's what you want then I'll make it happen."

"It is what I want, and I don't care what our parents think. We're putting ourselves first," she tells me softly before kissing my lips.

"Promise me that you don't resent me, promise me that this is truly what you want. Because I promise that I'm never letting you go."

She smirks. "You never did let me go, you were waiting, remember?"

I laugh because she remembers what I said once. "I'd wait longer if you needed me to."

Brielle shakes her head. "I've wanted this all along, it's just lately, I've been a bit down and lost sight of everything that is possible right now. It turns out, despite a minor blip in the summer, I'm one hell of a lucky girl."

"I think so too," I tease as I wrap an arm around her waist and slide her closer to me.

"Things out of our control made me question a few things lately, but I think we passed the challenge, because I'm still certain that you and I are meant to be."

Kissing her forehead, I smile because her words feel warm and right. "You sound very confident with your newfound happiness."

She pinches me in the side. "It's not new. I've been pretty damn happy since you tricked me into the middle of the lake. Only the universe wasn't letting me celebrate it, instead distracting me. I've lost a useless organ, among other not-so-stellar things."

"But you're at peace with everything? I mean, you've accepted that some things can't be changed?" This is me testing the waters.

"Yeah," she sighs.

Slowly, and reluctantly, I pull out the envelope from my back pocket. I look at it for a second. "Your results came in."

Disappointment floods her face. "It is what it is, I knew it would be any day now."

"Want me to open it for you?"

She holds my arms tighter as she leans her head against my shoulder. "Might as well get the confirmation." She sighs and looks out onto the ice.

I rip the seal and pull out the official letter and skim the lines. "It was a 266 that you needed to pass, right?"

"Yeah. I was aiming for 310, though."

"You know, I love the number 69 for many reasons," I comment.

"God, I did that badly?" She seems to accept her remark.

A giant grin spreads on my face. "I would say you have officially gotten everything you've been waiting for." Her eyes snap in my direction, and she studies my face. I hold the letter up. "You got 269, baby."

Her mouth opens, and I can see the utter shock spread through her body. It takes a few beats before happiness hits her cheeks. "What?" She grabs the letter in disbelief.

"You're pretty badass. I mean, you literally passed the Bar while your appendix was about to burst."

"Barely passed." She reads the paper in a hurry.

I scoff. "Babe, you passed, and I'm sure any future employer will accept your battle wounds for the explanation for your score."

It finally seems to hit her when happy tears begin to fall down her cheeks. She throws her arms around my neck, and I hug her until I think I might be crushing her. Rubbing her back, I soak in her embrace because this is the fucking cherry on top.

We both get everything we wanted. No concessions or almosts.

I swipe her hair and place kisses around her face, with her arms clinging to me.

"Oh my God, I was not expecting this. I guess I got lucky since it was the multiple-choice section where I went haywire."

"Or you are just amazing."

She creates some space between us and wipes away a tear. "This is…" No words come to her. "How did you have this, anyway?"

"Don't hate me, but I made Connor check the mail every day and hide it. It arrived yesterday. Not a fucking chance was I going to let you open it alone."

It earns me a quick kiss. "We have so much to celebrate now."

"You're telling me. In case you forgot, you said we're getting married soon."

"Oh, I didn't forget. I also didn't forget what I already had planned for tonight."

"Tonight? What do you mean?"

Brielle flashes me the sexiest look. "I believe my idea was after you put that ring on my finger that…" She toys with me by playing with my t-shirt, gripping the fabric at my chest. "Finally, I open the bag from a special boutique here in Lake Spark."

I growl at the image in my head.

———

I STAND OUTSIDE my bedroom door for one final check, examining the engagement ring that I plan on putting around Brielle's finger for the last time. This poor object probably needs clarification, since Brielle and I have been skirting around the lines of officially and unofficially being engaged

Smiling to myself, I open the door, and my eyes roam from the floor up to my bed where the only woman I need is splayed out in a way I've never seen her before. My dick instantly twitches from the sight.

Her brown locks splayed out on the pillow, a bra with lace and pink edging that only highlights the curves of her breasts. The panties match, but I have no plan on keeping those on. It's the suspenders with stockings that have me torn. The heels are just plain common sense to keep, as I have every

intention to fuck her and make love to her tonight. But hot
damn, those suspenders. I love Brielle naked, but I think I
want to keep those on.

She beckons me over with her finger. "Care to join me?"

A whistle escapes me. "You're… wow."

"It's different."

Very.

Brielle has always been confident on the intimacy front.
Yet, this set-up demonstrates a different era. We're experi-
enced, explorative, and exceptional with each other. If this is
any indication of married life, then we better speed up that
marriage license.

I crawl on the bed, coming to lie on my side next to her,
and my eyes dip down to really study her body.

"Can't believe you kept this from me."

"I wanted a special occasion," she whispers the reminder.

That's my clue.

"Finger," I order.

She holds up her left hand, and I slide the ring down her
finger. "Promise me two things."

"Anything," she rasps.

"One, you never take this off." I touch the new accessory
on her hand.

"I promise."

"And two. If anyone asks, especially our son, we officially became engaged on a rowboat on Lake Spark and not
in bed with you completely ready to undo me in sexy-as-fuck
lingerie, knowing damn well that I have every intention of
spanking you at some point this evening." I'm dead serious.

She laughs and brings her hands to the back of my neck to
play with my hair. "Totally promise on that. Now kiss me."

One kiss. Two kiss. A third.

Quickly, I rise onto my knees and peel off my shirt before

my jeans go too. My eyes never leave my fiancée who is watching me with a twinkle in her eye, her fingers exploring her own body and driving me wild.

I need to get my lips back on her, she's my lifeline.

Back on my side, I begin to toy with the tiniest of bows between her breasts, and I hiss a breath because she really is a vision.

I rub my thumb across her bottom lip, and she takes my digit into her mouth to suck, making a point to swirl her tongue around.

I take a deep breath to calm myself down. "You have a few ideas in that head of yours, don't you?"

"Uh-huh," she hums before sucking hard.

Her lips pop off my thumb, and she slides down the mattress, eager to pull my length out of my boxers and stroke me first with her hand, and then her mouth is covering me.

"Fuck," I curse as my head falls back onto the pillow. My fingers weave through her hair as she brings me to the back of her throat. Her sound of enjoyment and eyes seeking approval cause something feral inside of me to unleash. I swipe her hair to one side and pull it into a ponytail that I wrap around my hand, guiding her down on me.

I would be concerned by her slight gag if it weren't for the fact that her delicate hand grips tighter around my base and her tongue glides along my length. I don't want to go savage but the idea of a little drool rolling down her chin has me eager to postpone lovemaking until the next round, because first I need her to beg while she's in this little outfit.

Brielle doesn't relent and continues to work me with her mouth, but coming in her mouth just won't do. Pulling her off me, I gently toss her to the side of me on the mattress, and I'm over her in a flash.

Her legs are already twisting around my waist to pull us

flush together. My hand moves with speed, coasting down her body, until I find a strap from the suspenders that I snap against her skin.

She squeals and wiggles underneath me. "Uh-oh, have I been bad?" She plays along with a fun smile on her face.

My hand is back by her wrist to pin above her head. "Nah, you're the image of the kind of woman I want to marry."

I can't get enough of her. As if the atmosphere in the room is drowning me, and the only way for survival is to run my lips down her body.

I grab hold of her bra strap between my teeth, dragging it down and causing her nipple to peek out, then I'm on that with my mouth. I'm being pulled in all directions, losing my mind.

Then I feel her hand with the ring on my cheek. She draws my gaze to meet her eyes. "Ford, inside of me now."

Who am I to deny us that?

A few moments later, I'm inside of her with our hips rocking and lips sealed.

Sometimes in life, we get lucky, and it's only better when what you get has been in front of you all this time, taunting you until you have it.

———

WALKING out of the flower shop, I make a mental note to tell my sister that it's for sale, as she mentioned opening a flower shop after she graduates. She suggested I grab begonias for Brielle, and I had no clue what they were, but looking down at the soft, round pink flowers, I see her point. The color matches pretty much anything, including my jeans and white buttoned-down shirt.

Taking a few steps down Main Street, I grin when I see Spencer leaning against his sports car with his hands in his jeans.

"What brings you here?" I wonder.

"Baseball season is over, and I heard I need to run into town to pick up champagne for my neighbor."

I smirk to myself. "Oh yeah? Why would that be?"

"He has something to celebrate because his plan seems to have worked."

"Still pissed you didn't get an invite?"

He waves a hand at me. "Nah, intimate is more your thing. Doesn't mean you won't have cake and champagne waiting for you. Staying at the Dizzy Duck Inn?"

"Yeah, thought it would be good for a night. Violet will take Connor."

Spencer smiles gently with an affirmative look. "Do everything that I would do when I stay there."

I snort a laugh. "Didn't you make a certain kind of video there?"

"Good times," he reflects to himself with his gaze focused in the distance.

"I should go, I can't be late," I mention.

Spencer steps forward and slaps a hand on my arm. "Congratulations."

"Thanks."

A few minutes later, I'm sitting on a bench outside the courthouse.

"Are you sure you're okay with all of this?" I ask my son.

"I get to miss school, so yeah."

I place my hand on his shoulder. "That's not why we are doing this."

He flashes me a cheeky smile. "I know. It's just a bonus."

"A serious moment now. Man to man. All good? Your mom and me are about to become husband and wife."

"Kind of too late for me to say no."

I ruefully shake my head. Connor enjoys messing with me, yet his smile says the truth; all is well.

We both look up when we hear the patter of heels to find Brielle in a knee-length white dress. I notice some lace around the neckline, with her hair down the way that I like it. It's simple, but her.

I stand to hand her the flowers, and she seems appreciative.

"Ready?" She smiles.

I chuckle under my breath as I offer her my arm. "That shouldn't even be a question."

We decided to keep it as simple as possible. Celebrate between the three of us, relying on the courthouse staff to act as witnesses to keep the invite list small. Connor has been waiting for this day too, he was watching us all along.

This was a last-minute wedding, because we wanted to marry quickly, but it's a long-planned intention that's been floating in our minds for years.

Heading into the courthouse, hand in hand, I'm almost certain that as painful as it is, our journey was always going to be our way to this very moment. And perhaps that just makes it all the sweeter.

EPILOGUE: BRIELLE

SIX YEARS LATER

Summer in Lake Spark always causes my heart to beat in a different way. I know it's not physically possible, but it feels like it could be. It's as if memories and hopes dictate the beat of my heart. Or it simply could be that the season tends to put people in better moods, and I'm no exception.

It's the weekend, which means Ford doesn't need to check in at the training center, and I can leave my cases on my desk, as real estate law has statistically been awarded the least stressful of law practices, and that's what I picked.

I bring the tray of burgers and hotdogs to Ford who is manning the grill, with our new yellow Labrador Puck drooling as he sits in attention. I'm surprised he can still sit, as Ford has him playing frisbee constantly. We're throwing a BBQ with Spencer and April while Connor has a pool party with a few friends.

As I set the plate down next to the baby monitor because our three-year-old, Wyatt, is napping, I feel Ford's arm wrap

216 EVEY LYON

around me from the side so he can keep me close. I watch Ford give a steely stare at the pool of teenagers while his lips wrap around the bottle of beer. It causes me to smirk because I know what he's thinking.

Spencer arrives at the grill station with a chip in his hand, and he too notices Ford's tense study of the pool. "What's up with him?" Spencer bites the chip.

I chortle a laugh. "There are girls here," I note.

My theory about my son has been proven correct. The girls love him, and he's already playing for the varsity hockey team at the local prep school. The odds of popularity are in his favor.

"I thought you two have the whole 'we're cool parents because we're young' philosophy going." Spencer uses air quotes.

April laughs and comes to his side, bouncing their toddler son on her hip. "Don't you dare. You completely freaked out yourself when you heard Hadley talking about which older boys would be here," April warns her husband.

Spencer's face drops and his nostrils flare slightly. "I blame you two if shit goes down." The humor is there which makes us all smile.

Yet Ford hasn't broken his gaze on the hormone-fueled kids in our pool. "Nah, we're relatable. Connor knows he can talk to us about anything." I snort a laugh because as much as you can be close to your child, they will always try something behind your back, it's part of growing up. Ford glances over his shoulder at me. "What? I would rather they all do stuff under our noses instead of God knows where. Besides, we get them used to hanging out with us so they party here and keep it safe. We'll be those parents that even his friends want to talk to." Ford is confident with his approach.

"Smart thinking, actually," Spencer compliments. "Just

keep those hockey players from his team away from my daughter." He points at Ford.

"Likewise, keep those ballerinas away from my son," Ford counters.

April and I give one another a knowing look, and we gently shake our heads.

"By the way, where is your sister?" I wonder.

Violet moved permanently to Lake Spark a few years ago and took over the flower shop in town. It's kept her busy, and we love having her around.

"Late as usual, probably." Ford begins to throw the meat on the grill.

I tap his shoulder with my hand. "Come on, why don't you let Spencer take over for a little bit? I'm sure April will keep him in line." I smile at my friend, and she grins in agreement.

Ford blows out a breath and sets the tongs down in defeat.

We walk to the dock to get a moment alone. The afternoon sun always calms us.

"You okay?" I ask and rest my head against his shoulder while we look out over the lake.

"Sure. Completely. Yep." He smacks his lips together.

"So unbelievable," I add on, trying to suppress my grin. Ford is as tense as the times when my father comes over for dinner. Although the relationship between us all has improved, especially when Wyatt came into the picture, there will always be a wound.

He sighs and his arm hangs around my shoulders. "Want the truth?"

"Always."

"I'm fucking terrified that we are at the point where we have to worry about everything that could alter Connor's life from his choices." Ford seems agitated.

I do see the look of fear on his face, but it only makes my mouth stretch. "Trust me, I worry every day. *But* he'll find his way, and we'll be there for him without question. We promised him."

Ford exhales loudly, and I feel him relax slightly. "You're right."

We both sigh. When Connor was twelve, Ford overheard Connor talking with a friend about his first kiss, and then man-to-man, Connor told Ford. I'm not supposed to know. It was a girl from his music class at a party. I can only imagine where we are four years later.

"Life is good, Ford," I remind him.

He moves because a side embrace simply won't do. He needs both of his arms around me, and I won't ever complain about that. He lowers his mouth to capture my lips for a kiss.

"It really is," he confirms with a whisper. "I love you."

"I love you too."

One of his hands sneaks between us and he places the pads of his fingers on my belly. Instantly, I grin in pure bliss.

"We'll be doing all of this again in sixteen years."

My eyes peer down between us where my husband is touching my pregnant belly. "We'll be pros by then." I'm only halfway, and we just found out that another little boy is going to enter our lives, which Connor very much approved of, as he loves being a big brother and can't wait to train his own little team of hockey players.

Everything is different pregnancy-wise these days. Planned pregnancies, for one, but we also have everything we could possibly want or need to make this smooth sailing.

"How are you feeling?" Ford's attentive eyes search my face for a true answer.

"Perfectly okay. I took a nap earlier, and now I'm kind of starving."

He kisses me fast and hard. "We better get you fed then." Taking my hand in his, he tugs me along back to the seating area. "Spence, how are the burgers? My wife needs her protein."

A spray of water comes out of April's mouth, and she dives her head into Spencer's shoulder to maintain herself. "You should totally know by now that Spencer and I take that sentence completely out of context."

Spencer shakes his head.

Ford laughs and continues on with his mission by grabbing a plate. "You two always liven the party, that's for sure."

My attention on my friends is broken when the sight of a puddle appears at my side, I smile when I see Connor standing there and drying off with a towel. "Mom, where's Aunt Violet?"

"Good question," I reply. I'm fairly confident he talks to his aunt about girls, and I'm sure she is more updated than we are. I hum in response. "She'll be here soon."

"Uhm, Brielle, can you help me with the pasta salad that I brought?" April interrupts us.

My eyes draw a line to the table, and I swear I see the pasta salad there and ready. Looking at April, she is giving me wide eyes and the indication that the pasta salad is a cover.

"Right, salad. Kitchen?" I suggest.

She nods. I quickly kiss Ford on the cheek who is now in a deep conversation with Spencer about sports.

A minute later, I find myself in the kitchen where energy springs into April's body, and her face tells me she is excited. "I can solve the mystery of where your sister-in-law is."

I lean against the counter. "Violet?"

April nods. "I was at the grocery store and heard the old lady from the knitting club tell the cashier that she saw the florist canoodling with some new guy in town. Naturally, I turned to Hadley who was at the ballet studio near Violet's flower shop, and she confirmed that she saw a guy talking to Violet."

I'm intrigued. "Okay, and?"

April's face brights up. "It was a guy with a Maserati." My face stays blank.

I scratch the back of my head, because I'm hearing the story, but something still doesn't connect.

"Brielle, figure out who has the Maserati, and we solve the mystery."

"Or I just ask her."

"It's more fun playing detective."

I peer over her shoulder to see that Violet has arrived, and Ford is already getting her a glass of wine.

"Come on, she'll tell us if there is something to tell."

April groans, as if I am ruining her entertainment.

I interlink our arms and yank her with me back outside to join the group.

"Hey, Vi, we have plenty of food, so help yourself," I offer with a smile.

"Thanks. Sorry I'm late, it was a busy day at the shop."

"Normal busy or unusual busy?" April questions.

I give her a death stare.

"Normal busy, I guess." Violet doesn't take notice as she fills her plate with food.

Glancing around our backyard, I see the guys already offered hotdogs to the kids who arc now sitting over on the dock with their legs hanging in the water while they chomp on food.

"We're going to need to throw on another round. Those boys are growing," I comment.

Ford leans over to kiss my cheek. "I'm a step ahead of you. Besides, we have more adults joining us."

"I thought Hudson and Piper went to see his son in Blue-top," I say.

Ford grabs the bowl of salad that I still have not perfected cutting. "They are, but I invited Declan. Now that he owns the Spinners and is adamant that they train here in Lake Spark, he'll be around more."

I hear someone nearly spit out their drink, and my head whips in Violet's direction.

"Are you okay?" I ask.

She pats her chest while her hand returns the wine glass to the table. "Yeah, totally, just drank a little too fast." Her attention turns to Ford. "Around more?"

"Declan? He's thinking of moving here," Ford answers.

Her face drops as the sound of a car motor hits my ears. My focus on Violet is broken when one of Connor's friends who is walking into our yard hikes his thumb over his shoulder calls out, "Con, your parties are always unreal. Not only are the adults here like former pro athletes, but now you have a guy show up in the newest Maserati, and I'm pretty sure he looks like Declan Dash." The teenager shakes his head with a grin.

My eyes snap to April who looks thoroughly satisfied, before my sight pins to Violet who is holding onto her wine glass for dear life as she hides behind another sip of the expensive white.

Mystery solved.

The thing about Ford is that he is a caveman when any man comes near me. When someone goes near his sister? He is a bear, and not the cuddly kind.

This isn't going to end well…

THANK YOU

To my readers who give me the drive to keep writing, a big thank you.

Lindsay, I've lost count how many books we have gone through now!

Autumn, thank you for making my insanity a little more…sane. You're the first eyes on the book and I'm oh so lucky.

To my little family, we're going strong. Thank you for allowing my ridiculous coffee runs and writing times. But writing about hockey players who fall in love is essential for the world to turn!

Made in the USA
Middletown, DE
18 August 2023